THE VAMPIRE OF SIAM
RAMONNE

JIM NEWPORT

Encyclopocalypse Publications
www.encyclopocalypse.com

BOOKS BY JIM NEWPORT

The Vampire of Siam

Ramonne: The Return of The Vampire of Siam

The Reckoning: A Tale of The Vampire of Siam

Chasing Jimi

Tinsel Town

The Siamese Connection

A Dark Christmas

PRAISE FOR JIM NEWPORT

THE VAMPIRE OF SIAM

"Grand Guignol entertainment…good for nibbling on the beach."

— *JAMES ECKARDT, THE NATION.*

"Chilling and morbidly hilarious. Newport's intimate knowledge of the Far East makes this an ultra-realistic journey into terror."

— *PULITZER PRIZE NOMINATED AUTHOR CHRIS BUNCH.*

"Well-researched, engrossing, smart and sexy. A graveyard smash."

— *BOBBY 'BORIS' PICKETT, SINGER-SONGWRITER: THE MONSTER MASH.*

Rating: 5 stars

— *JOHN WALSH, MANGO SAUCE.*

RAMONNE

"Newport retains, from his first novel, a sharp sense of place for modern Bangkok. This is the trendy Bangkok of the Emporium Suites, the skytrain, the Q Bar, the Bed Supperclub."

— *THE NATION.*

"Newport artfully adapts the vampire legend into a Mekong cocktail of surprises."

— *CHRISTOPHER G. MOORE.*

THE RECKONING

"Newport's novels succeed in their purpose: they entertain."

— *THE NATION.*

"The books are rich in cinematic imagery...and fascinating details of Thai history."

— *THAILAND TATLER.*

CHASING JIMI

"Did you miss the 1960s? This funny yet loving and respectful adventure mystery will take you back."

— *JERRY HOPKINS, AUTHOR OF THE DOORS: NO ONE HERE GETS OUT ALIVE.*

"Newport has gone from the vault of the dead to the electrifying life of Jimi Hendrix. If you can remember Woodstock, you will enjoy this book."

— LANG REID, PATTAYA MAIL.

TINSEL TOWN

"It moves like a runaway asteroid."

— TIM HALLINAN, BESTSELLING AUTHOR OF
THE POKE RAFFERTY SERIES (SET IN BANGKOK).

"Tinsel Town is the best introduction-to-Hollywood novel I've ever read."

— DAVID GILER, PRODUCER/WRITER OF THE
FILMS ALIEN, UNDISPUTED, MYRA
BRECKINRIDGE AND MANY MORE.

THE SIAMESE CONNECTION

"Jim Newport is a writer with great skills. Non-stop, hold your breath action. A true thriller. "

— LANG REID, PATTAYA MAIL

"Newport clearly knows Bangkok…An easy read."

— BERNARD TRINK, BANGKOK POST.

ACKNOWLEDGMENTS

I would like to thank the following for making this book possible:

Boyd Willat for believing in me; Christopher G. Moore for leading me down the path; Uraiwan Kotatha for lighting the way; Hubert, Manat and the people of Kamala for their hospitality; Ben Howard at Shrimp Asia for the graphic design; Patrick Gauvain for the expensive wines; Tim Young for the cheap booze; and David Johnson and the staff at Asia Books for their support.

Quotation from "Werewolves of London" used by permission of the authors: Waddy Wachtel, Leroy P. Marinell and the estate of Warren Zevon.

"I saw him in the bar at Trader Vic's...and his hair was perfect."
Warren Zevon

The Vampire of Siam
RAMONNE

VoS 2

1
———

Johnny Boy opened a bottle of Cristal champagne, poured it into a fluted glass, and moved across the marble floor, his doeskin slippers making hardly a sound. He sat on the white Corinthian leather couch, one of a half-dozen matching pieces. A polar-bear rug and the pale floor were in sharp contrast to the jet-black sky outside the floor-to-ceiling windows and doors at the room's end. 'Gangster chic' they called it in L.A., the other City of Angels.

The Emporium Suites was the address *du jour* in Bangkok—thirty stories of gleaming glass, steel, stone, and marble above the up-scale Emporium shopping center, next to Benjasiri Park —and Johnny Boy Lao's penthouse would rate a video crew and a spot on MTV's "Cribs."

Outside, beneath him, were the eternal city lights of Bangkok.

Millions of fairy lights entwined the columns and cascaded from the canopy of the building, and in the small plaza outside the department store entrance, conical shapes swirled to form a thirty-foot tree of lights. It was Christmas.

But it was always Christmas in Thailand.

Johnny Boy drew a silver Haliburton case from beneath an

I

alabaster coffee table, spun a three-digit combination, and snapped the locks. Emerald re from within cast light across the flat lenses of his Armani spectacles. He ran a hand through his oiled hair and then chose a walnut-sized gem from the viridescent pile. He emitted a low whistle as he held the stone up to the beam of a tensor lamp and marveled at the purity and clearness of the color.

White fingers encircled his dark hand and delicately removed the stone.

"*Suay*." The girl put the precious gem to her lips and lightly kissed it. "*Suay maak maak*."

"Yes. Very beautiful. Like you." Johnny Boy smiled and replaced the stone in the case. He took the girl's hand and placed it on his lap. Her fingers flicked the drawstring of his silk pants and the knot came undone. He leaned back on the couch and sipped his champagne as she slid the silk down his thighs.

A warm, gentle breeze blew across his skin, causing his ne body hairs to stand and his attention to wander to the windows.

The doors were open and the white curtains billowed beside them.

"What the fuck?" Johnny Boy propped himself up on the pillow and stared. The windows were never opened. He could only tolerate Bangkok's locker-room humidity in the constant presence of bone-chilling air conditioning.

———

He pushed the girl aside and reached under his pillow. He racked a round into the chamber of a silver .45 automatic and sat up.

"Did you open the window?" He looked at her.

"No," came the timid reply. She stared as he pointed the pistol and walked to the end of the room. He stepped through the open doors and onto the terrace. Thirty floors below, a stained-glass canopy shielded a pair of gold Rolls Royces whose very presence raised the monthly rent by 20,000 baht.

"The maid must have left it unlatched and the wind blew it open," the girl offered.

What fucking wind? Johnny Boy shrugged as he closed and latched the doors. He retraced his steps, slipped the pistol back under the pillow, and pulled the slender girl to him. She resumed her exploration of his manhood, taking him between her lavender glossed lips. He moaned and tilted his head back on the pillow, squeezing his eyes shut as ripples of pleasure spread in waves.

When he opened his eyes, he saw *him*. Seated in a leather armchair, his face obscured in shadow.

"Lord Buddha." Johnny Boy grabbed for the pistol, the startled girl falling indelicately to the floor. He leveled the gun at the figure in the chair.

"Who the fuck are you?"

The figure didn't move. It continued to stare from the shadows.

"Answer me before I blow your fucking head off." Johnny Boy leaned forward with the gun.

finally the figure spoke: "You didn't finish."

"*What*? What are you talking about?"

"The sex act. You didn't finish it."

Johnny Boy looked down and realized he was exposed and still erect. Embarrassed, he pulled up his pants, drew the string tight and knotted it.

The figure leaned forward into the light and Johnny Boy got his first glimpse of the man. "You *must* finish. It leaves you all backed up. It's not healthy, you know."

The man was European, mid-thirties, handsome with longish hair that curled at the collar of his silk suit. A shock of pure white, an inch wide, ran through his raven locks. "Please." He gestured to the girl. "Continue. Our business can wait." He leaned back in the chair and crossed his legs.

"Our *business*? I ain't got any business with you. Except blowing your fucking head off. What are you doing in my damn house anyway? And how did you get in?"

The man looked at the glass doors. "Bullshit. We're thirty floors up."

"Actually, I came down from the roof—"

The doors slammed open, smashing into the wall and shattering the glass.

The girl shrieked and jumped next to Johnny Boy on the couch. She shivered and clutched his arm.

"I've had enough of this bullshit. Fuck you." Johnny Boy fired point blank at the man's heart.

In a move too fast for the human eye, the man's right hand was in front of his heart, palm out. Upon impact the hand closed, but the force of the blow knocked him and his chair off balance. He recovered and brought the legs back down. He took his closed fist away from his heart and opened it. A flattened .45-caliber slug lay within.

The girl sank to her knees. She began wailing, her hands pressed to her forehead. Johnny Boy just stared

"Put the gun down."

Johnny Boy laid the gun on the coffee table and the man placed the slug next to it.

"What do you want?"

"You've been a very bad boy, Johnny. My client has lost patience with you."

"Your *client*?"

"Ping Narong."

"*Ping*? He sent you?" Johnny Boy smiled and sank back on the couch. The girl continued to whimper and he gave her a swift kick. She stopped. "Ping and I have a long relationship. He's an *old friend*."

"He no longer considers you a friend. As I said, he has lost patience with you." The stranger stood over the coffee table. He was six feet, lean and muscular. "That's why he sent *me*."

Johnny Boy stood. Physically they were well-matched. "Listen. I know Ping's got a bug up his ass about me. He thinks I've been stealing from him."

"He *knows* you've been stealing from him. I know you've been stealing from him." The stranger's eyes bored into Johnny Boy, who could *feel* him in his brain.

Johnny Boy shook his head and it stopped.

"Look, Ping's an old man. His time is past. I represent the future. My time has come. You look like someone I could use. Work for me." Johnny Boy poured a glass of champagne and held it out for the stranger.

The stranger scowled. "Your time is up."

He smashed the glass from the outstretched hand and leapt for the gangster's throat. His powerful jaws sliced through the man's larynx and a crimson tide soaked the white shirt.

The girl shrieked hysterically. The man stared at her while he took the young gangster's life, and she became quiet.

The death dance took just a minute, and the stranger released his bite and let the corpse fall to the floor. He turned his attention to the girl. She whimpered as he put his hand into her black hair and stroked it. He heard a sound and looked down. A stream of amber fluid was running from her onto the marble. It made a small pool near her feet.

He smiled and whispered, "You saw nothing. You were not here."

She nodded and retreated to the front door. He surveyed the room as she slipped into the foyer and the private elevator. She collapsed as the car descended.

The stranger picked up the Haliburton case and the gun. He placed the pistol into the dead man's hand and curled a finger around the trigger. He raised the muzzle to the gash on the throat and pointed upward. The gun discharged, taking the top of Johnny Boy's head off. He let the hand with the pistol drop to the floor.

He walked to the terrace and looked down over the railing,

watching until the girl appeared and got into a cab. He looked up at the lighted columns of the roof, swung the silver case in an arc and let it fly. He waited for the *kerchunk* when it landed on the roof, climbed onto the railing, and leapt straight up. Twenty feet. He grabbed the strut of a huge arc light and swung himself up and onto the roof, where he picked up the case.

On the far side, he dropped twenty stories onto the roof of the Emporium shopping complex. He waited for a skytrain to pull into Phrom Phong station and then dropped onto the pedestrian bridge, blended with the crowd, and disappeared into the night.

———

Martin Larue reached into his tattered canvas bag and retrieved his only worldly possession. A key.

A key.

But it was another key that he had been in search of for the last year. The key to life itself.

The Way. The Path to enlightenment.

The Noble Truth.

But this key marked his return. Open this door and shut all others.

He ran a hand over the stubble on his "large American head," as it had been described at the temple by Noi, a white-robed novice *mae chi*, or 'nun.' Her head had also been freshly shaved, but somehow the body/head proportion seemed more Godly and less grotesque than the watermelon with ears he had seen in the chipped and cracked mirror that first morning a year ago when his head had been shaved to minimize personal cares and worries. In all his years, Martin had never before cropped his hair. It was also the last mirror he saw for a year.

The doorman at the apartment building on Soi Lang Suan bowed in reverence to the orange-robed monk when Martin approached. But there was no predicting the reaction when Martin smiled and asked to be let into the building.

"Khun Martin. Is it really you?"

Martin smiled. "Yes, Pom, it is I. The prodigal son has returned."

Security guard Pom *waied* and opened the doors to the lobby.

"I heard you had gone to the temple in search of the light, but I did not believe it."

"It's true. I sought, I found, I've returned."

Pom pushed the button for the eighth floor and backed away, continuing to bow.

————

The key opened the teakwood door. He resisted stepping across the threshold. Resisted stepping back into that world; the world he had rejected.

You are your own master.

He slipped out of his sandals and stepped into the room. The tile in the entry was cool on his calloused feet. The drapes were drawn and the room was pleasantly shaded. He moved a hand across a wall panel and soft lighting came on. An air conditioner hummed to life. He switched it off. He crossed the room, parted the drapes, and opened the French doors to the terrace to let the air in. He gazed for a moment at the children at play in Lumpini Park, flying kites, chasing a ball, skipping stones across the lake.

Each time one of the pebbles broke the water's surface, the attending ripples seemed to spread across the lake in a rainbow of color.

He shook off the memory and turned back to the room. The maid had been in attendance and everything was clean and dust-free. He moved to the bookcase and its eclectic display of artifacts: carved wooden Aboriginal sun lizards, Maori tattoo needles and mallet, tribal masks from New Guinea, Noh masks from Japan, Balinese shadow puppets, and native American *kachina* dolls. A tribute to a life spent wandering the globe. A life free of financial concern.

One month shy of his graduation from Harvard and entry into the real world, Martin's father passed away, leaving Martin the sole heir to a fortune so vast he would need eternal life to spend it all. Oddly enough, in his adopted home of Bangkok, he had met a true vampire who almost granted him just that. Ramonne Delacroix's 175-year-old *visions* were so seductive that Martin almost allowed himself to be transformed. Eternal damnation, he realized, was what awaited. When he came to his senses, he had joined forces with an American vampire hunter to destroy the charming beast.

They literally destroyed the vampire. Martin had stood on the hallowed ground of Wat Arun and blown the monster's head to bits with a single shotgun blast. He kept vigil over the headless corpse until the sun rose and incinerated it, the wind blowing the ashes into the mighty Chao Phraya River.

Martin picked up a photo in an art deco frame. He and a willowy Thai woman, dressed in formal attire. They beamed at the camera.

Daeng. His girlfriend for five years.

When the bitter smoke from the vampire's funeral pyre had finally dissipated, Daeng was gone. She'd had enough; enough of his patronizing attitude, his ambivalence, his infidelity, and, certainly, enough of the madness that had allowed him to consort with a vampire.

It was the loss of Daeng that had pushed Martin over the brink. He had closed the door and walked away from his luxurious lifestyle with nothing in his pockets but a single key.

For twelve months he had studied the Middle Way. Learned the Noble Truths. Practiced the three fundamental principles: Not to do any evil; to cultivate good; to purify the mind.

He'd gone to Wat Nong Pah Pong, upcountry in Ubon province and prostrated himself before the *ajaan* and requested sanctuary and the glorious opportunity to study the *Dhamma* of the great Teacher, Buddha. He would forego all worldly possessions and pleasures. He would not imbibe of food after noon, and would be dependent on the kindness of others for all his needs. He would spend his time in meditation, not speaking at all for at least three months, as was this temple's policy.

He was given three orange robes, a candle, and an empty rice bowl.

Martin had wept openly as his head was shorn, the tumbling locks representing to him all that he had lost in his life of excess and the selfish pursuit of sensual pleasures. That night and every night for the next three hundred and sixty five days, Martin slept like a baby.

———

A buzzer went off, startling Martin. He wasn't sure what the sound meant. He'd gotten used to temple bells, gongs, and chimes. It buzzed again and he recognized it as the house phone. He picked it up.

"Yes?"

"Khun Martin, you have a visitor."

Already? "Who is it?"

"Lieutenant-Colonel Samarat. Police"

Another buzzer. More pleasant in tone. Martin knew it as the doorbell, and opened the door. In the hallway a thin man in a tight brown uniform was crushing out a cigarette in a cylinder of sand, and he spoke without looking up.

"Martin Larue, I'm Lieutenant-Colonel Samarat from Bangrak precinct—

He stopped dead at the sight of Martin in his monk's robes. Quickly he put his palms together, pressed them to his temple, and bowed.

"I'm sorry, your holiness. I am here to see the *farang*,"

he said in Thai.

"I am not so holy and I *am* the *farang*. Please come in," Martin replied in Thai.

"Khun Larue?" The colonel puzzled as he stepped out of his shoes and into the apartment.

Martin noticed that Samarat had addressed him incorrectly, by his surname, but said nothing. He nodded and led the officer to the terrace.

"I am only here temporarily, on this errand. I will offer you refreshment, but I'm not sure what I have."

"Water will be ne, thank you."

"I'm sure I can manage that. Excuse me." Martin went into the kitchen and emerged momentarily with two cold glasses. He placed them on the coffee table and sat in a bamboo lounge chair opposite the colonel.

The officer took a long sip while Martin sat in silence. Samarat placed the glass back on the coaster.

"Thank you."

Martin smiled and nodded.

"Khun Larue, I had no idea you were a monk."

"I have spent the last year studying meditation at Wat Nong Pah Pong. I have just this moment returned."

"I'll try to be brief. You must be tired."

"I *was* tired. Now I'm refreshed."

"Khun Larue, my predecessor, the late Colonel Boonsong, was involved with you, was he not?"

"*Involved* is an auspicious word, Lieutenant-Colonel. We were acquainted."

"You were with him when he was murdered, yes?"

"I was."

"As I understand it, his daughter was kidnapped and he died in a struggle with her captor."

"That's correct."

"Before Boonsong succumbed, he managed to fatally wound

the man, who fell into the river and drowned. His body was never recovered."

"Also correct."

"There are many unanswered questions in this case. The daughter has refused to discuss it, and you…well, you have been unavailable."

"Yes I have. But I must tell you, if your mission here is to discuss this 'case,' as you call it, you are wasting your time. I have built a wall between myself and that incident—a wall it took a year to build—and I will not let you tear it down."

Martin rose and started for the door.

"Good day, sir. I think I was wrong. I *am* tired now."

"Khun Larue. Areeya Boonsong's kidnapper was suspected of multiple murders. Murders in which the victims were drained of their blood. And now there are more!"

Martin opened the door. "Good day to you, sir."

Samarat crossed to the open doorway.

"The murders, Khun Larue. They have started again."

He stepped through the door.

"I need your help. If you have truly found the *Way*, then you know you must practice the three main virtues of the Buddha: wisdom, purity and compassion. Compassion includes social responsibility."

He slipped on his shoes and stood facing the American monk. "It could be said it's your *duty* to help me."

He handed Martin a business card. Martin took it, bowed and gently closed the door.

2

Residents of Sihanoukville have become alarmed at the disappearance of four 'sea gypsies'—fishermen that go regularly into the caves of Koh Kong to collect the bat guano. The men are normally in the caves no more than six hours, as the shifting tides can be quite hazardous. The cave is home to thousands of bats. When Kuk and Prei did not emerge from the caves after fourteen hours, their two brothers, Pol and Tong, went in search of them.

That was over two days ago. The captain of their boat returned with an empty craft and immediately went to report the incident. Captain Ravang of the Koh Kong police said that a 'rescue party' was being organized and would depart at dawn.

When questioned, the boat captain offered another strange postscript to this tale. Bats, being nocturnal beasts, are normally out of the caves at night, which is when the men went in for their usual gathering. But with each entry into the caves—first with Kuk and Prei and then Pol and Tong—there was a loud noise within the cave, indicating that some of the bats were still present. Also, when the normal droves of bats did return at dawn, their numbers were greatly reduced. Strange things afoot (or should we say aloft) in Koh Kong.

———————

How odd to sleep upside down.

Hanging by your claws.

Claws?

How odd to have claws.

And wings.

How odd to be alive—if that's what this pitiful existence was.

His brain was small. He awoke initially with but a dim memory. Blurry radar-screen images of another world. A world other than this enormous cave.

He awoke ravenous. Instinct kicked in. He fed on his fellow cave-dwellers. They were terrified of him. He fed and fed.

And he grew, to ten times the size of his little brothers and sisters.

As he continued to gorge and feed and grow, the memories came to him…He had once been a *man*, not this leather-skinned, winged animal. He was born a long time ago in a distant land. But his real life had begun 143 years ago in a ruined temple, not far from his current home.

He was an explorer, on a mission to document wildlife on the Mekong River when, quite by chance, he came across the wondrous ruins of ancient Angkor Wat. Driven by a mad desire to see the magnificent carvings, he had gone with a torch into the Temple of Bayon. There he was set upon by an ancient beast, a 1,000-year-old Chinese vampire. Weakened by hundreds of years of feeding on nothing but livestock, the ancient vampire was too feeble to take away his life. Instead, the attack left him transformed into a fellow bloodsucker. Together they decimated the human contingent that had been his comrades just days before.

Wandering west he came to the great port of Krung Thep, the capital city of Siam. With his heightened abilities—physical strength, telepathic powers, and perpetual youth—he reveled in all the pleasures and splendor that the great kingdom had to offer at the end of the nineteenth century.

On into the twentieth century, he continued to reside in the city, now known as Bangkok, finding its legions of lost souls the perfect food source for his ravenous appetite.

But shortly after the dawn of the new millennium, he made the mistake of forming a bond between himself and a mortal. This ultimately led to his downfall. To his demise.

Now, this being with pointed ears puzzled at this, as he rested in his chamber, hanging upside down over the rotting remains of hundreds and hundreds of his fellow bats. He was now the size of a dog. A small labrador.

If I truly met my demise on that fateful night at Wat Arun, what am I doing here, in this terrible reincarnation?

Then he heard the voices at the entry to the cave. If it were physically possible, he would have smiled.

No matter.

He knew it was just a matter of time before he would once again regain his human form.

Once again he would be...

Ramonne.

———

The sleek 'cigarette boat,' hidden near the entrance to the cave, bobbed gently with the undulation of the sea. The full moon glinted off the water as it began its descent, barely an hour until dawn.

Kanchana lit another cigarette, the third in a row.

It must be tonight. All the signs are correct. After tonight the moon will be on the wane.

She could not afford to wait another thirty days.

She didn't have another thirty days.

At dusk, she and the boat's owner had watched as the police boat pulled up and six armed men had stepped into the cavern. Some were drunk, and they pitched their empty whiskey bottles into the sea. She heard their voices as they joked and cursed on their way into the cave. Then she heard a great shriek. Then screams and gunfire.

Then silence.

That had been over ten hours ago.

He has fed well. He must be strong now.

It was thirty days ago that Kanchana had brought the tiny creature with its very special DNA to the cavern and released it. Since then she had read the reports of the sea gypsies' plight and had known what had happened.

It is as the shaman had predicted.

He would feed first on his own kind, and then on the auspicious offerings of the fishermen. Gradually he would be restored to his human state. But the shaman could not predict with accuracy when he would be fully restored. Only that his removal from the cave would have to occur within the full moon. What Kanchana would find in that cave was unknown. A man-beast? A hybrid of man and bat? She shuddered and clutched the talisman that the shaman had given to her for protection.

This is insane. But only the truly desperate know the depths of their own insanity.

Kanchana had found hers, and as the first soft hue of dawn started to color the night sky she motioned Yon to prepare to enter the lair.

Yon started the motor and they slowly proceeded to the mouth of the enormous cavern. The empty police boat was moored outside.

Just inside the cavern, a series of poles were lashed to a stone ledge. Old truck tires were attached to the pilings. Yon tied off the boat and shut the engine. Kanchana was about to climb onto the makeshift pier when Yon grabbed her and pulled her down.

"*Lang.*" He pointed back to the mouth of the cave where a black cloud suddenly appeared. A swarm of bats, returning from their nocturnal raids, swooped into the cave. The movement of air and the noise of their flapping wings frightened Kanchana and she cowered in the boat. Within minutes, all but a few stragglers had returned to their nests deep within the cave.

"Best to let them sleep, before we enter," Yon offered.

"Yes. Of course." Kanchana realized how much of this 'plan' she hadn't thought through or anticipated.

Like the police showing up.

The fishermen were certain to enter the cave. That was a given. On the eve of the full moon. It was their job. Their territorial right. Paid in blood by their families over the centuries.

But the police and their 'rescue party'—this was something else. She was terrified when she saw their boat arrive. They could spell the ruin of this. The creature's strength was unknown. He could only possibly be overwhelmed by the police.

But if he had been, she reasoned, then surely the rescue party, whoever survived, would have emerged by now.

While she pondered this, Yon gathered his gear—his torch, rifle, and ropes. The long crate Khun Kanchana had placed on board in Bangkok lay nestled in the bow. He'd been paid more than a year's wages to make two trips to Koh Kong. The first, a month ago, to deliver an infant bat to the cave. And now this journey, to retrieve it.

What all the fuss was about over one tiny bat, he couldn't imagine. But the woman had insisted from the moment she boarded in Klong Toey that he wear an odd silver amulet as protection. This had disturbed him. Protection from what? She had merely smiled and clutched the matching talisman that adorned her slender neck.

A great clamor came from deep within the cavern. Hundreds of bats screamed in unison. Instinctively Yon shined his torch into the cavern.

Something was there.

Kanchana followed the torch's beam.

"*Look*."

A figure stumbled through an inner arch and collapsed on the wet stone floor.

Kanchana's heart sank. It was true, after all. They had beaten the creature.

She was finished. Even if this was the only member of the police force left alive, the answer was the same. The creature was dead.

Cautiously, Yon made his way to the figure. He held his torch in front of his rifle. What he saw as he approached sent a shiver through his bones.

"Khun Kanchana," he called out. "It's not the police."

"Who is it?" She stood up in the boat.

"I don't know. You should come." Yon continued to play his light over the figure. It moved in spasmodic jerks.

Kanchana stepped onto the ledge and took two steps toward the arch.

Immediately she knew it was *him*. She almost fell to her knees in gratitude, but she proceeded until she was standing over the wretched creature.

He was more man than beast, but nature still had its grip: The ears, yellow eyes, canine fangs. Hair covered its naked back and legs. The hands and feet were bent into impossible claw-like appendages.

Cracks and groans were heard from within the creature's tortured body as its metamorphosis continued before their very eyes.

Beast he might be, but Kanchana recognized the man in its face as it writhed in agony.

Yon stared in wonder as the woman pressed her palms together and tilted her head to the sky in silent prayer.

———

The sun was a big red ball starting to disappear as the boat motored up the Chao Phraya River. The journey from Koh Kong had taken all day. The seas in the Gulf had been calm and Yon had managed to stay far enough away from shore to avoid all police activity. What they would make of his bizarre cargo, if they checked, he had no idea, and he had no desire to find out.

In the cave, he had lashed the thing's feet and hands and dragged it to the boat. He opened the wooden crate and, to his amazement, found an elegant coffin. Its interior was lined with silk. He started to ask why, but Kanchana looked at him and shook her head. He remembered his place, and that he had agreed to not ask questions, but merely to obey her requests, no matter how bizarre. For this he was paid, in advance, a small fortune. Enough to keep his little family—wife and two infant children—fed, clothed, and housed for a year. In these troubling economic times, Yon thanked Lord Buddha for the day Kanchana walked into the boatyard and Khun Prang had assigned him the job of ferrying her to Koh Kong in one of the finest boats in Prang's small fleet. Loading the comatose thing into the coffin and shutting the lid was merely one of the rich woman's odd demands.

Yon fingered the amulet she had insisted he wear. A kilometer south of the Taksin Bridge, Kanchana motioned for him to turn west into a small *klong* leading to the exclusive homes of Thonburi. Yon had once piloted a tourist boat, and he remembered the guide explaining to the daytrippers how you could tell a rich area by the grooming and condition of the dogs that yapped at them from the docks. In contrast to the scruffy street mutts that one encountered on the Bangkok side of the river, the dogs of Thonburi were purebred, freshly shampooed, and fattened up on the kind of food the poor would be glad to get their hands on. The poor lived by the river, bathing and washing in it, their wood and tin shacks crowding the edge of every *klong* in Bangkok. But the homes that these fancy dogs pranced in front of were set back from the canals, with high hedges and fences and broken-glass-topped walls guarding their privacy.

The houses all seemed to glow with the same warm light reflecting off their varnished teak walls. The private docks were strung with lanterns and, as the sun departed, the canal took on a magical quality.

The boat glided for ten minutes until Kanchana pointed out a green pier jutting from one of the more lavish homes. She motioned for Yon to stop. He pulled the boat up to the landing and shut off the engine. Two servants appeared and helped him tie off the craft. There was a block and tackle rig on the pier that was used to raise and lower outboard motors and small crafts. Kanchana motioned and one of the servants swung the boom out over the boat and Yon ran two canvas slings under the wooden crate. The servant turned the crank and lifted the box from the hold and swung it onto the pier. A metal gurney awaited it, and the two servants wheeled the crate up a stone path to the house. They departed without having uttered a single word.

———

"Will there be anything else, Khun Kanchana?" Yon asked.

Why the lady had asked him to remain, he didn't know, but he had waited patiently on the dock for over an hour, busying himself with cleaning the boat. When the lady emerged from the house, she was alone.

"No thank you, Yon. Your service has been quite satisfactory."

Yon thought she would say more, but she remained silent.

"Thank you, Khun Kanchana. If ever I can be of service to you again—"

"I know where to find you." Then she held out her hand. Yon was puzzled. She pointed to the amulet he wore about his neck.

"Oh yes. I'm sorry, I forgot." He untied the leather thong and handed it to her.

She smiled. "One more thing, Yon. I have to be able to trust that you will tell no one of what you have seen on our journeys together."

"You have my word, Khun Kanchana. I will not tell a soul. I'll take your secrets to my grave."

"Yes. Of course you will. Thank you." With this, she turned to the house and walked down the little path.

He watched her depart, then turned to the boat. He was unlashing the bow line when he heard footsteps on the grass. He turned and was knocked to the ground.

The naked, now fully formed man tore into the hapless boatman. Before Yon could utter a cry, the man attacked, severing the jugular vein.

Ramonne gorged on the warm rich liquid. His magnificent muscles rippled as a fine sheen of sweat began to form over his chiseled body. A white streak ran down the center of his long hair.

Finished, he flung the boatman into the *klong*. He then stood fully erect and shook his body like a dog, sweat and blood flying in droplets.

He smiled as he clenched and relaxed his fists, feeling his strength. He not only felt good…he felt reborn.

He reached down and undid the boat's mooring line and watched as it started to drift down the canal. Then he looked at the mansion and its promise of a new life.

3

Kanchana Sorhiran had seen death before. She'd watched as first her grandmother, a great aunt, and then her own mother succumbed. Her parents had hidden the gory details from the young girl, but the grief and terror had been unbearable. Each woman had lingered and suffered for months.

Kanchana and her mother had been extremely close, especially since her father had taken his own life, rather than bear witness to more intolerable suffering. But even her own mother's painful demise had been shielded from Kanchana by the staff of servants, nurses, and doctors who administered to her.

Then it was the act of nursing her sister that brought home the terrible reality of the disease and its inevitable progression through all female members of the Sorhiran family in the last fifty years. It terrified Kanchana and drove her to desperation in a search for any way to avoid the plague she would soon succumb to.

She personally tended to Prinsada, her sister, in her last days. She saw the fungus growing from her eyes and nostrils, smelled the air of decay, and witnessed the horrible transformation of a once beautiful woman into a withered husk. Her every breath was filled with agonizing pain and misery.

Modern medical science had no cure for Kanchana. Only medication for the pain. Bandages for the blisters and sores. Only ointments and salves, pills, injections, saline drips, intravenous feedings, and, finally, mind-numbing opiates for the last days of the rampaging disease.

But no cure.

And so Kanchana turned her back on medical science and went to the *other side* in search of help. She turned to witchcraft and sorcery. The black arts.

In Bangkok, a city where the locals knew that ghosts were real and 'witches' brewed potions aimed at keeping evil spirits at bay, it was rumored that one could find a cure for anything.

Even death.

Kanchana's servant, Loh, was the first to mention the shaman's name: Charoen.

Kanchana had politely dismissed him until the hundredth trip to another specialist yielded the same prognosis.

———

Shortly after nightfall on the eve of a full moon, Loh had guided the woman through a labyrinth of shops and stalls on the fringes of Sanam Luang, the royal cremation ground. Tables groaned with Buddha images in gold, silver, and wood. Cases displayed amulets with the Teacher's image embedded in glass vials. The symbology became phallic as they plunged deeper into the maze. Wooden penises of every size and shape guaranteed fertility. Next came the herbologists. Dispensers of snakes suspended in jars of brine. Geckos and lizards, pressed and dried. Bones, whole and crushed. Monkey skulls, tiger penises, and bear paws.

Nearly a half-mile into the bazaar and Kanchana was reeling from overexposure. Loh had assured her they were almost at their destination. She smiled and steeled herself to carry on.

Soon, all pretexts of religion or medicine were dismissed as the alleyway opened onto a small *soi* of two-story shophouses overlooking a narrow, fetid *klong*.

Unlike every other *soi* in Bangkok, there were no noodle vendors or 7-Elevens on this street. Beaded or bamboo curtains obscured the entry to most of the shops, and Kanchana caught fleeting glimpses as Loh led her down the dusty street. Bare fluorescent tubes in pink or red flickered in a few interiors, but most were dimly lit by candles. A 'gypsy' woman, with large hoop earrings, turned cards. She caught Kanchana's eye and beckoned for her to come in. Loh warned her away.

At the end of the *soi*, a silver Mercedes was incongruously parked in front of a typical shophouse. The entry was open and a small man lay in a hammock. A young girl and an older woman, both well-dressed, sat opposite him. Candles burned on the low table before them. The man sipped tea from a small glass as he gently swayed. The young girl was nervous and the older woman held her hand.

Loh motioned and they stopped. They stayed in the shadows opposite the parked car and watched.

Though they could not hear the dialogue, it was obvious to Loh what was happening. "The young girl worries about her future. Will she have a happy marriage? Her mother has brought her here to find out. Though blind, Charoen sees all."

Kanchana had cringed. So this was the famous Charoen. Her savior was blind.

She studied the little man as he spoke quietly to the girl. Though his shoulder-length hair was gray, it was impossible to tell the shaman's age. His dark skin marked him as a southerner. He was dressed in loose-fitting black pajamas. His head rolled from side to side as he talked, his sightless eyes squeezed shut as he concentrated.

This had gone on for twenty minutes, an eternity to Kanchana. Finally Charoen was finished and the two women bowed before him, their hands pressed to their foreheads in a very reverent *wai*. The shaman sat up and returned the *wai*. The mother opened her purse and started to hand him an envelope, but Charoen waved to a servant who bowed and took the envelope. A driver held the door for the two women and in a moment they were driving away.

The servant helped Charoen out of his hammock. It appeared they were about to go inside when the shaman turned in the direction of Kanchana. He opened his eyes and smiled. His eyes, devoid of pupils, were pure white. Without speaking, he called Kanchana to him.

———

"I first heard that there was a powerful *phii dib* in Bangkok five years ago. The ghost who drinks blood was rumored to be somewhere in the Bangrak district of the city, preying on prostitutes and other denizens of the night. Lost spirits constantly wander in search of their eternal souls, and the missing connection that will allow their return to the wheel and the cycle of reincarnation. But this spirit was rumored to be a *farang*. And very old: 175 years.

"I was intrigued. If in fact he was foreign and as old as they said, then this was no ordinary *phii dib*, this was a real vampire. A truly forsaken one, cursed with all the powers of the undead."

Charoen, Kanchana, and Loh were in the upstairs living quarters, surrounded by jars and bottles filled with unspeakable potions. Candles burned in every corner. They sat at a large table, sipping a potent tea that was constantly replenished by Charoen's servant. Charoen appeared to have switched to whiskey, which he mixed with water.

"Years passed and the rumors grew, but I had no contact with the mysterious beast. Then one day a police colonel brought his reckless daughter to see me. As is my way, I touched the girl and then the father, getting a mental picture of them. The girl was the typical child of a strong authority figure:

spoiled and rebellious. But the man...I was almost burned by his touch. He was steeped in evil and graft, his soul virtually divided by his public role of the people's defender and his private forays into hell. But, sad to say, this was also typical. What caused my excitement was the feeling that this mortal was in contact with, somehow *in legion with* the vampire."

While they talked, Charoen's servant had brought a small straw-woven box. He placed it on a side table.

"I wanted to query the policeman about the forsaken one, but knew that he would deny any knowledge. Instead I sent Jar to spy on him. Within days Jar reported back with the most amazing tale. It seems that the vampire kidnapped the police-man's daughter and demanded a ransom. Further complicating matters was the appearance of a vampire hunter. I foresaw the endgame and dispatched Jar to bring me a piece of the vampire. A lock of his hair, a fingernail, anything—so that this being's power should not slip through my grasp."

A sound like *scriiit!* came from the straw box and Kanchana jumped. Charoen smiled and continued his tale.

"Alas, the dance of death took place on the grounds of Wat Arun, and Jar watched helplessly from the opposite bank as both the police colonel and the vampire were destroyed."

Kanchana had felt uneasy. She shifted in her chair. "Khun Charoen, fascinating as your tale is, I fail to see its relation to my plight. Forgive my curtness, but my time is short—and precious."

"I am well aware of your plight, dear lady. I know of your inescapable fate."

"I was led to believe that you could help me."

"I cannot save you, dear lady. There are other shamans who would gladly take your money and pretend to cure you." He had motioned to the street below. "Knock on any door on this *soi*."

"Then why—"

"*He* can save you. *He* can offer you eternal life. It is your only chance."

"But you said he was destroyed."

"He was. Jar witnessed the decapitation and the incineration of the body."

"Then how—"

Charoen held up his empty hand and smiled. "Jar is a faithful and loyal servant. He had a mission. At dawn, he joined a group of monks who were ferried to Wat Arun for morning meditation. Jar scooped a handful of the vampire's ashes."

A small silver vial appeared in Charoen's hand. He handed it to Kanchana. She opened it.

"It's empty." Charoen smiled.

"It is. I have taken the ash and made a powerful potion." He opened a narrow box next to his right hand and produced a syringe. Reflexively, Kanchana rolled up her silk sleeve and extended her arm to the shaman. The sightless man smiled again.

"No, my dear. This is not for you. It is not that simple."

He pushed down the plunger and a drop of fluid shot out.

"The vampire must bite you. He must draw your blood. But he must not kill you. Then, on another night, he must bite you again. It is this second bite that will transform you. That will grant you eternal life. A life free from all pain, all decay. You will remain as you are...beautiful...forever. But there is a *price*—"

"I don't care what the price is. I will pay anything." Again the shaman smiled. "You will pay me a significant sum, that is true. But this is not the price I am referring to." He nodded to Jar, who brought the straw box over to the table.

He lifted the top. Inside was a creature. Barely the size of a field mouse, with large ears and wings.

Jar held the tiny bat while the shaman injected it with the hypodermic. The bat emitted a shriek and then was immediately calm.

It was as if it sensed the destiny it had just been given.

4

Three hundred and sixty five nights of deep, uninterrupted sleep. And now, one night in his own bed and Martin could not sleep.

It was impossible, of course. Martin had pulled the trigger and watched the sun take his friend's body.

His *friend*. That was how he would always think of him. Bloodthirsty, demon-spawn that Ramonne was. To Martin he had offered his gift.

Oddly enough, the vampire had engineered his own demise. He had laid a path to a vulnerable location, through the kidnapping and ransom of a corrupt man's daughter. When Martin and Jonathan Peyton—the vampire hunter turned vampire—attacked Ramonne, he quickly dispatched Jonathan and relished in the slaughter of the police officer.

Then he turned. But instead of attacking Martin, he revealed the fact that he was prepared to sacrifice his own existence by choice. He had grown weary. Weary of the game. Weary of the hunt.

He was willingly offering himself up for slaughter.

The monster, it seemed, had gained a conscience—a very heavy burden for a vampire. Subsequent to this soul-baring confession, Martin was never sure that he had actually pulled the trigger of his own free will, or if, in fact, Ramonne had willed it through his telepathic powers.

But this much Martin did know: Jonathan Peyton, unwilling vampire who never tasted human blood, requested and was granted a blast from Martin's shotgun.' Both bodies were gone in the morn.

Decapitation on hallowed ground and subsequent incineration by the rising sun guaranteed the vampire's true and total demise.

Could there be another vampire stalking Bangkok's twisted maze of back *sois* and dens of iniquity? Certainly among the thousands of victims Ramonne had taken throughout his long and checkered life, the possibility existed that one had survived to receive the fateful second bite and fallen to the dark side.

No. One thing that could be said about Ramonne: he was thorough. Competition was not part of his nature.

Martin turned and tossed.

Perhaps this was merely a ploy of this new lieutenant-colonel to uncover facts in a case that should lay buried. Perhaps there was no bloodletting; no new victims drained of their blood, as he had said.

In any case, it could not possibly be Ramonne—and therefore it was none of Martin's business.

————————

Interior vice minister Surapol Padahum was tired. He'd had a long week. Putting the squeeze on Phuket to clean up its tarnished image was exhausting work. He and his entourage had staged raid after raid on the three-block stretch of Soi Banglah. By week's end, at least half the go-go bars were shuttered tight, temporarily, until the fines could be worked out and paid. The Barracuda, one of the most popular discos—foreign-owned; one of Surapol's personal pet peeves was the foreign ownership of so many venues in the 'entertainment zone'—was permanently shut down, its German owner cooling his heels in the Phuket jail for a series of Polaroids found in his office featuring naked girls in an after hours party.

The usually half-naked dancers in the bars that did remain open, like the Rock Hard A-Go-Go, now wore so much spandex that they looked like they were doing aerobics in a fancy Bangkok health club, rather than gyrating in a tropical sin palace.

Work, work, work. Arrive unannounced and corner the patrons with the help of the local gendarmes. Single out the foreigners for on-the-spot drug tests. Getting a urine specimen was never a problem; *farangs* all seemed to drink gallons of beer. Order the holding of their passports until the test results. Stiff fines for those caught under the influence of drugs. Stiffer fines and closure of the clubs caught serving drug offenders. Comb the premises for lewd behavior. The finding of a single un-used condom in the lavatory of one club was cause enough for its foreign owner to lose his license and hence his livelihood.

Restore order to the realm: That was the prime minister's crusade, and Surapol was up to the task. In a land known for its anything goes attitude, bars, restaurants, discos, every place, now shut their doors promptly at 1:00 a.m. Never mind the protests of the taxi drivers, bartenders, waitresses, and restaurant owners that they were being driven to the poor house, the policy was clear and the law was the law.

Surapol leaned back in the plush interior of his bulletproof Mercedes. The vice minister had received numerous death threats. The latest was rumored to have been offered by a notorious Chinese Mafia lord with his tentacles into every corner of Thailand's teeming market for sensual pleasure. A bounty of 10 million baht for his head!

Surapol smiled at the amount. A worthy testament to his good work. Still—he fingered the 40,000-baht chain around his neck—good to keep one's head firmly on one's shoulders. The custom vehicle was one way of securing his safety.

Another was the contingent of armed bodyguards who accompanied him wherever he went. Rak and Jobi, his two toughest men, rode in the car with him, packing Uzis. The other four rode in two additional lead-plated vehicles. With the good vice minister's car in the middle they formed a procession that was virtually impenetrable. He was immune to the black-visored motorcycle assassins who were often the last sight for many of his political comrades. The vehicles were swept for bombs before each and every departure. The vice minister's personal residence, where he resided with his frigid wife of thirty years, was also completely checked for incendiary devices at least twice a day, as was the house of his 25-year-old mistress, Joy.

Joy's house on Sukhumvit Soi 49 was the current destination. Surapol took out his cellphone and punched code 69, his own private joke, and waited while the line rang. In a moment he heard the sultry voice that never failed to set his loins on fire.

"Hello, *tilac*. Did you miss me?"

"More than you'll ever know," he cooed. The girls provided by his lackeys in Phuket had been too young, inexperienced, and clumsy. One had even had the audacity to bleed while he pummeled her for her poor performance.

So much for southern girls.

The cars left the expressway at Din Daeng exit. Surapol was in a jovial mood, joking on the phone, when the car in front swerved violently. He looked up to see a man attempting to cross the exit ramp.

Drunken fool.

Just as the vice minister's car drew level, the man leaped directly into its path. Surapol was thrown forward to the floor as the driver desperately hit the brakes. Then there was a tremendous impact followed by two thumps as the car rolled over the man. This was followed by a terrible *squealing* of brakes and then another impact as the car following them slammed into their rear.

Surapol cried out as Rak helped him struggle back to his seat. "Did we hit him?" As the words came out, he knew the answer.

Jobi, who sat in front and never wore a shoulder harness, was bleeding from a wound on his forehead where he had hit the windshield.

The driver, visibly shaken, pulled the car to the shoulder. The car behind, steam hissing from a punctured radiator, pulled alongside.

Jobi put a handkerchief to his head wound and stepped out. Surapol opened his door and leaned out to watch. The first car was backing up the exit as the two bodyguards stepped out of the third car. Rak remained in the car with the vice minister.

"Is he all right?" Another foolish question, Surapol realized. He had the cellphone in his hand and he suddenly remembered Joy was still on the line.

"What's happened?" he heard her say as he put the phone to his ear.

"There's been an accident. I'll call you back."

Jobi approached the crumpled figure. The man lay face down, his legs and arms twisted at impossible angles. He didn't move. Jobi bent and put a finger to the man's neck and felt for a pulse.

In a moment he rose and shook his head. "He's dead." Surapol slumped in his seat.

Jobi took a cellphone from his pocket and started to dial a number when suddenly the man began to stir. With a series of snaps and cracks, the legs and arms adjusted back to normal.

"Huh?" Jobi closed the phone and moved toward the man.

His face still turned away, the man started to rise. "Mister. Don't move. Stay still. I'll get help." Jobi opened the phone again, while the other two moved to restrain the man.

"I don't think that will be necessary." The man rose to his full height. He twisted and rolled his neck and another loud crack was heard.

"Ahh. That's better."

Jobi gaped in awe as the figure turned to him. Long black hair with a shock of white tumbled into his face, and he tossed it back, revealing eyes that glowed a bright yellow. He smiled, showing two elongated canine teeth.

"*Phii!*" Jobi dropped the phone and reached for his Uzi. Instantly the creature was upon him, ripping his throat with a serrated knife. Jobi slumped to the ground wordlessly clutching his severed larynx.

The two other bodyguards opened fire and the bullets tore through the man. He was bounced and rocked by the hits, but continued to move on them, finally ripping the weapons from their hands and gutting them both with the carving knife. Their entrails tumbled forth as they fell to the pavement. Rak opened his door and began to fire.

Ramonne, moving faster than the eye could see, threw the knife and it appeared in Rak's chest, to his utter astonishment.

Ashen faced and almost comatose with fear, Surapol managed to scream at the driver, "Go! Go!"

The driver, hands shaking, tried to put the car in gear, but Ramonne was upon him. He tore into the man's throat and began to drink his blood. Cars continued to stream past the scene. In Thailand, only the naïve and the half-witted stopped at the scene of an accident.

In the lead car, a decision was made. The doors slammed and the car screamed off down the exit.

As Ramonne finished with the driver, he looked into the back seat. Rak was in his last dying throes, his hand clutching the pearl-handled knife. In the corner, the vice minister cowered, his eyes bulging with fear.

Finally Ramonne released his grip on the lifeless driver. He stood and walked to Rak. He pried his hand off the knife and pulled it from his chest. Rak dropped to the asphalt.

"Please. Oh Lord Buddha, please. Spare me," Surapol begged as Ramonne walked around the rear of the car.

He smiled and leaned in to within an inch of the terrified man.

"Boo."

The vice minister shut his eyes and mumbled a rapid-fire litany of prayers as Ramonne reached in and pulled him from the car by his hair. He raised the blade and swung it in an arc. In one swift stroke he cleanly separated the vice minister's head from his body.

The two cars were both belching steam, and the tarmac was slick with the visceral ooze of the corpses as Ramonne, holding the vice minister's gaping head by its hair, strolled off the exit and disappeared into the night.

5

———————

What a *bitch*.

Ramonne watched Kanchana devour the young boy.

That's two in less than one hour. He shook his head in disgust as she wiped her lips with a silk kerchief and dropped it to the ground. She was walking away when he grabbed her arm.

"Dispose of the body." He picked up the kerchief and handed it to her. "And leave nothing of your own property."

She took the kerchief, folded it, and put it in her purse. "Thank you. I forgot. Could you get rid of him, *mon cherie*? I'm exhausted."

He knew she was anything *but* exhausted. He marveled every night at the increase in her strength and stamina with each successive kill.

He bent, picked up the body of the young man, and dumped it unceremoniously into the canal.

Women.

Ramonne had known many women in his life. And in the afterlife, as well. As a young art student there had been his beloved Giselle. She had been a mere waif of fourteen when he first met her. But over the years she became his model and the love of his life. So enchanted was he by her beauty that he produced dozens of canvases of her. Mostly nudes. But it wasn't until the young artist met Henri Mouhot—explorer, photographer, adventurer—and became Mouhot's charge d'affaires, that he could afford to treat his beautiful Giselle to the fineries she deserved.

They'd been married when he left the port of Marseilles one fateful morning in 1860 with Mouhot on an expedition to Indochina. The vision of her standing on the pier, tears in her eyes, was the last he had of her, for he was never to return from that perilous journey.

As a forsaken one, Ramonne had a sensual lust that was almost akin to his need for blood. He was in the habit of seducing young wayward girls of the night, sexually ravishing them and then, as they writhed in ecstasy under the tutelage of his powerful tongue, biting into their womanhood and drawing their life from them.

For Ramonne, educated, cultured, civilized gentleman of a bygone era, sexual pleasure was one of the last enchantments provided by a world that had slipped into decay and stagnation as mankind found more and more ways to numb the senses.

Kanchana was his benefactor; he realized this from the moment when he first laid eyes on her as the lid was opened and he stepped from the coffin into the parlor of her mansion on the *klong* in Thonburi. All that she had done to restore him to his physical state was revealed to him in moments. Her disease, its consequences, and her desperate plea to avoid that fate—all of this flooded over him in a wave of images as he stood naked before her. He knew he would embrace her desire and grant her request.

He had felt renewed and invigorated by his feed on the hapless boatman, but though she pleaded that time was of the essence, he was not in shape to take on her task. He feared that once he started to draw her sweet nectar, he would be unable to stop, and all her careful planning would be for naught as she would wind up as nothing but a pale corpse.

Instead Ramonne dressed in the perfect-fitting suit of clothes provided by Kanchana, had Loh ferry him to the Oriental pier, and by the first hints of dawn's arrival, when he returned to his coffin, three children of the night had met their demise and Ramonne slept like a fatted calf.

The next evening, in a four poster bed, draped with a white net and surrounded by dozens of candles, Ramonne sexually cavorted with Kanchana for three hours, taking her in every known—*and some unknown*—positions, before finally granting her the first non-lethal bite, administered to her thoroughly saturated mound of Venus.

He departed the boudoir, leaving the poor woman gasping for air and clutching the sheets. He locked the door and deposited the key in his pocket.

Loh had the boat ready but Ramonne was in such desperate need that he leaped across the *klong* and killed the first hapless soul he came across.

The next night, Ramonne unlocked the woman's bedchamber. She was asleep. He slid down the silken sheet and put his lips to her labia. Carefully inserting his canines in the small punctures, he started to draw her blood.

Instantly, she was awake. Her hands pressed on his head, while her back contorted to the breaking point.

After a minute, Ramonne withdrew. "No. Don't stop."

"No. It's enough."

He headed for the door. She grabbed his hand. "What happens now?"

"I don't know."

This was the enigma that was Ramonne. Suckled against his will in a Cambodian temple 143 years before and then set forth, undead, into a world of the living—knowing only that he must feed regularly on human blood and avoid the sun. In 143 years, he had never encountered another vampire—only the vampire hunter Jonathan Peyton—who Ramonne made a vampire by mistake. The rules of his existence, he learned through trial and error. Through trial and error he figured out how to survive and thrive in Siam.

The city he inhabited in 1860 was truly a magical place. Graceful crafts of every shape and size sailed the canals that laced one golden-spired section to another. The river was full of tall ships from all over the globe.

He slowly amassed a collection of art, books, and wines. He moved these into a succession of safe houses—usually the home of a lonely victim; someone chosen for their wealth, secluded residence, and solitary manner. Ramonne grew skillful at adopting his victim's personas—and their bank accounts—especially those foreigners whose untimely demise he managed to disguise from the gendarmes for years. Consequently, endowments continued and salaries were drawn.

There were even instances when Ramonne physically assumed the identity of the victim. One stroke of fate introduced him to a young Frenchman in a café near Hualamphong, the central train station.

The young man had literally just arrived, bags in hand. He was due to report the following evening as the booking agent of the new jazz club in the famed Oriental Hotel. Needless to say, that was the young man's last night on earth, and the next was the first of a ground-breaking run for Ramonne as the talent coordinator of the legendary Bamboo Bar.

Jazz aficionado that he was, Ramonne reveled in the serendipity that allowed him access to divas, horn players, pianists, all the greats of the time, and book them into his own little jazz bar. It was only when a relative of the young man's decided to visit the mysterious Far East that Ramonne reluctantly abandoned his post as the Oriental Hotel's resident jazzman.

Eventually, Ramonne found a secluded and forgotten

enclave deep within the bowels of Lumpini Boxing Stadium, and here he surreptitiously moved his collection of art, artifacts, books, and wine.

He settled in to an anonymous existence and bided his time. He enjoyed what vestiges of the old world still existed. Bangkok was at its best, a melting pot of the old and new, and he remained a spectator as the twentieth century merged into the twenty-first.

It was the eve of the multi-hyped, highly-anticipated New Millennium that sent Ramonne on a self-destructive bent that he would not—in fact, did not—want to recover from. He watched from the rooftop of the Bangkok World Trade Center as thousands of drunken, drug crazed, lonely people forced themselves to celebrate, forced themselves to participate socially. An art form that was lost on them.

If there was one thing Ramonne regretted most about the times he witnessed, it was the great isolation that modern man had imposed upon himself. People no longer gathered in outdoor cafés or met evenings in the village pubs, but instead they stayed home, captivated by technology: Bright screens that emitted information written in binary code, and badly edited Hollywood 'claptrap.' The great 'dumbing down' of the masses' was well underway.

Ramonne had watched from his lofty perch as the New Year revelers celebrated their great non existence. His fury with the mortals' ignorance was such that he went on a rampage, devouring and decimating scores over the five-day holiday that Thailand celebrated.

And then he met Martin.

Martin. Martin. Martin.

The only man he'd ever loved. Martin, the mortal who had got under his skin.

Martin, the only one in 140 years to uncover his existence.

Martin, possessor of a fortune vast enough to sustain 'eternal life.'

Martin, curious enough, keen enough, and jaded enough to keep up with the vampire's nightly forays.

Martin, the first mortal to whom he voluntarily offered the *gift*.

Martin, the one he betrayed.

Martin, the one who made him finally realize that this Godforsaken life of wanton destruction was worthless…loveless…lifeless.

It had been Martin that had ultimately led him to decide to orchestrate his own demise.

The mortals believed they were in charge, believed they pulled the trigger, when in truth if Ramonne had not consciously decided to escape the foraging and plundering that had gone on for over a century, they would not have stood a chance. He could easily have destroyed them.

Instead he voluntarily walked into their trap at Wat Arun and allowed himself to finally be sent to hell.

Or so he had thought.

What a rude awakening that had been. *A bat. A rodent.* Possessor of a pea-sized brain. Trying desperately to process the DNA that held Ramonne's 175-year existence.

And the pain.

The rebirth had been painful beyond description. Rebirth was not a request that he recalled making.

But now that he had returned, Ramonne vowed to make the most of it.

———

Fuzz. Stubble. Three days growth.

Three days of indecision. Lost in his thoughts. The thoughts he'd been taught to control were now flooding over him.

It was time to make a decision. Time to return. Martin had come home for one reason. Now, that reason would make him stay.

He put down the razor and ran his hand over the stubble.

One decision made.

And one decision led to another. He picked up the orange robe from the chair where he'd left it, and placed it in a maple drawer. He opened a wardrobe and chose a white cotton shirt and a pair of tan linen trousers.

Today Martin would rejoin the world.

———

"A year. I can't believe you actually did it. I can't last a week without getting laid."

"Some things are easier to give up than others. I actually missed my morning oatmeal laced with honey more than I missed the company of women."

Rejoining the world for Martin meant rejoining his social circle. A few phone calls and dinner arrangements were made. La Scala, a new Italian bistro at the elegant Sukhotai Hotel was the chosen venue. John, a Brit who covered the politics of the kingdom for the German press was seated next to David, an ice-cream heir and part owner of two go-go bars in the infamous Nana Entertainment Plaza. Although Martin was not imbibing, a bottle of shiraz was already finished and they were only on their appetizers.

"But there *are* female monks aren't there?" David motioned to a waiter for another bottle.

"There are a few *nuns*, yes, but as you can imagine, they keep their distance. Apart from the first day when I had my head sheared and there were nuns in attendance, I didn't have contact with a woman the whole time. As you know, a woman is not allowed to have any physical contact with a monk. Even offerings of food or alms must be placed in a bowl or on a cloth, but never offered up directly."

"So, Martin, are you gay now?"

"No." Martin smiled. "Just happy."

"Touché." John raised his glass in toast.

"*Chok dii.*" Martin returned the toast.

"What are your plans now?"

"I don't know. Travel maybe. I haven't decided."

John shook his head. "Tough life. Decisions. Decisions. Doesn't it ever bother you that most of us have to work for a living?"

"John—" David tried to cut him off.

"No. Let him answer."

"Of course it does. That was one of the reasons for my going into the monastery. What's it all about? Why me? What's my purpose here?"

"And? What's the answer?"

"I don't know." Martin smiled. "But when I do, John, you'll be the first to know."

Martin raised his glass and John reached over and rubbed the stubble on his head. "You know I missed you, you twit."

"What *really* happened?"

"Again, I'm afraid I don't really know, David. A nervous breakdown, I guess."

"Come on. Don't give us that crap," John chimed in. "Nervous breakdowns were what our mysterious nutty aunts had when we were kids. Not guys like us. We OD on booze or drugs."

"You know I don't drink or do drugs."

"Another mystery about you. All the money in the world— you could be swimming in Dom Perignon and have all the 'top drawer Turkish embassy' hash in the world if you wanted. How do you do it?"

"Do what?"

"Stay straight in this fucked up world?"

"Come on, John. You're missing the point. Martin has a story to tell."

"I wish I did."

"Martin, for fuck's sake, we're your mates. You were acting

like you'd seen a ghost. You drove your fucking girlfriend bonkers with your late night magical mystery tours and tales of bloodsucking French aristocrats. And then you joined the monkhood. Now what the fuck was it all about?"

Martin tried to avoid their eyes. He knew it would be like this. He just wasn't ready for it. Not yet. "I told you. I had a nervous breakdown. Started seeing things. Imagining things. It was the monastery or the loony bin. I chose religion. I confronted my demons in solitude: I found myself again, and now I'm back."

"End of story?"

"End of story."

"Then I say welcome back. And as a bona fide, dues-paying member of the Siam Society, the City of Angels officially welcomes you back." David offered up another toast.

Martin raised his glass of soda water and saluted. "It's good to be back."

Their main course arrived and Martin dug right into the succulent lamb chops with a fury that impressed John. "Whoa! I guess monk food isn't all its cracked up to be."

Between mouthfuls Martin said, "You're at the mercy of your constituency. You make your morning rounds with your empty rice bowl. I wasn't in a particularly wealthy village and the offerings were fairly modest." He chewed and swallowed. "On the plus side, I dropped twenty pounds."

They continued their meal in relative silence, each savoring the excellent cuisine. When they finished, John ordered a brandy and pushed back his chair.

"Strange the current upsurge in violent crime, here in the land of smiles, eh?"

David nodded knowingly.

Martin was at a loss. "What's going on?"

"Hard to say. Some of it looks like gang warfare. Some of it looks the work of a particularly ruthless assassin."

"The Surapol thing was fucking amazing," David offered. "Couldn't have happened to a nicer cunt, I might add."

"Spoken like a true smut purveyor."

"I beg your pardon. That's 'publican' to you."

"What happened?" Martin asked again.

"He was literally beheaded. His whole entourage, except for two smart lads who fled the scene, were butchered. They claim it was one lone assassin. Stories going round of machine-gun bullets going right through him."

Lord. I am not ready for this.

"Then there's Johnny Boy Lao. Small-time hood in a big racket with expensive tastes. Slaughtered in his thirtieth-floor penthouse All the doors locked tight. No one entered the building. All the monitors showed nothing."

Oh no, please. Not again.

"And just like the driver in the Surapol thing, there was no blood in the body."

The room started to spin. Martin put his hand to his head, just to hold it onto his shoulders.

It's true. He's here. It's impossible.

"Martin are you okay?"

Oh yeah. Just okey dokey. Hunky fucking dorey. "Yeah. Just a little too much civilization, a little too fast. Excuse me."

Martin got up and walked down the hallway. The stone *chedi* reflected in the still pond reminded him of the quiet nights in the temple.

Once inside the bathroom he immediately vomited the expensive meal.

He looked into the mirror. The face that looked back was unrecognizable. He'd aged ten in the last year. His short stubble of hair made his ears seem enormous. The lines around his eyes and mouth were like the river flows that etched the Grand Canyon. His tan was so deep that he had the color of burnt coffee.

What am I worried about? He'll never recognize me.

The ridiculous nature of the thought hit him immediately and he collapsed to the floor—alternately laughing and crying.

Recognize me? He reads my damn mind.

"Jesus, man. Are you okay?"

John had just walked in and discovered Martin.

"Oh yeah. Just fine."

———

Thonburi, Ramonne decided, wasn't big enough for two vampires. He'd tired of being Kanchana's nanny. He taught her what he knew. She now slept in the basement of her house in an elegant metal coffin. Fireproof. The door was firmly secured against intruders.

"How will I know when it is night?" She worried.

"Don't worry, you will."

The amulets that Kanchana and the hapless boatman had worn were unfamiliar to the vampire, but he sensed their power. *There is so much I need to know.* They were sealed in a strong box and dumped in the canal by the faithful Loh.

Loh was now completely under the vampire's spell, and performed whatever was asked, without question and with complete discretion.

Without the spell, Ramonne feared that the she-devil, as he now took to regarding Kanchana, would one night devour the helpless servant in one of her feeding frenzies. The spell also protected Loh as well as indenturing him.

Ramonne, the ultimate loner, preferred solitude, but he knew she needed the servant to survive. The woman was strong, and beginning to get her wits about her after the initial shock of her transformation had worn off.

She was eventually able to think of things other than blood-letting. She even expressed interest in reviving her social life, though this, Ramonne warned her, was potentially fraught with peril.

"Do you have a lover?" Ramonne asked her.

"Only you, *mon cherie.*"

They sat in the garden of her mansion. A full moon illuminated her collection of Greek busts and the night air was sweet with the smell of jasmine.

Ramonne studied the head of Aristotle as he quietly lectured her.

"You must be very careful. You won't be able to control yourself. Any foolish romantic notions you entertain will be destroyed in front of your eyes by your own hand. Believe me, I know."

Kanchana laughed. "Perhaps that is not so bad. Variety is the spice of life."

She sounds like me. But why shouldn't she? She's a fucking vampire. Again Ramonne shuddered as he considered the potential of the beast he had truly created.

"Believe me. This is not funny. You must exercise discretion." *Discretion? Did I really say that?* "Your survival depends on anonymity. Travel in your old social circle risks exposure. Do you think that they won't notice the change in you?"

"My dear, I'm toying with you. I understand the need for discretion. But there is no fear, as I will have you to guide me." She slipped her arm through his.

He slowly, carefully removed it. "No. No you won't. I'm leaving."

"What?" She hissed. "Leaving *me*? I gave you back your life. A fortune has gone to your resuscitation."

"I didn't ask for it. I was content to be dead. You, on the other hand, did beg me to save your life. That I did. Now you must go down your own path."

"*Mon cherie,* don't. Please—"

"This is for your own good. Do you realize the carnage *two* vampires would cause? Do you think it will go unnoticed? If we separate, we have a chance."

I should destroy her right now.

But how? Ramonne did not have the answer.

"Stay on the Thonburi side of the river. Have Loh dispose of your victims. I have instructed him. He will see that you survive. Trust no one else."

Ramonne turned and walked up the path to the dock. He did not turn back.

She was a vampire. She would not beg.

In the moonlight Kanchana saw the silhouette of a boat. Loh stood on the pier and Ramonne climbed into the craft. From the way it rode low in the water, she knew that his coffin was already on board.

Red streaks ran down her face as she watched the boat motor away into the night.

6

Such nonsense. Ramonne watched the 'future boy' work his magic. *Just like Tommy — the 'deaf, dumb, and blind boy.' How can he be saved from the eternal grave?*

See me. Touch me. Heal me.

Ramonne was so amused by the shaman's control over these lonely souls, that he actually allowed two girls to plead their case and have their 'future' foretold before he grew impatient enough to send the second one packing.

"Please, sir. I've paid a lot for this reading."

Ramonne's steely gaze told her that any more argument would be fruitless. Downcast, she *waied* the spirit man, her hands pressed together high on her forehead, and headed for her car. Charoen's servant stopped her and handed back her money.

Ramonne watched the BMW drive down the dusty *soi*.

"At last we meet."

Ramonne looked around the room, wary as always.

"Don't worry, my friend. No one will harm you here."

"That I do believe," Ramonne replied. "But it is knowledge I seek. Not sanctuary."

"It is knowledge you shall receive. This I assure you. Please come in."

Tommy, can you hear me?

Ramonne crossed the threshold into the gnome's parlor of potions.

"Please sit down."

Books. Where are the books?

"It is an honor to have you here. You are the culmination of my search."

"Your search?" Ramonne shifted in his chair, curious.

"Yes. I have dreamed of the day when I might meet one with your powers."

Ramonne was already bored by the little man. "You have a library, don't you?"

"Yes. A very special one. Unequalled, I'd dare say." He rose from his chair. "Come with me."

Ramonne followed the blind man up the stairs to the second floor of the shophouse, where he was confronted by a multitude of books. All in Braille.

The shaman smiled wickedly. "I will be glad to be your interpreter."

Ramonne picked up the first volume.

How odd.

He had never seen Braille before. He gently ran his hand over the dots and dashes. To his amazement, the text came alive in his hand. He smiled. "Actually. I don't think that will be a problem."

Ramonne sat in a chair and passed his hand over the title page:

Sorcery, Spells, And Incantations.

Interesting, but not exactly what he was looking for.

The little man smiled as he went to the shelves and pulled out two tattered, leather-bound first editions. "I'm afraid that the modern world has totally denied your existence. These tomes perhaps hold the answers to your questions."

Ramonne took them and studied their titles. *Vampires And Vampirism* by Dudley Wright. Published in 1914. The second was Reginald Hodder's *The Vampire*, published in 1912. He had heard of both books. Both were very rare and, in the fruitless attempts he'd made over the years to find answers, they'd been unavailable to him. He opened Hodder's book. Immediately he was engrossed in the fifteenth-century tale of the infamous Vlad Tsepesh, or 'Vlad the Impaler' as he was known.

Soon, the shaman's house, the street of spirits, Bangkok…in fact the whole world, ceased to exist as Ramonne became completely absorbed in a world of folklore, mythology, and hypothesis.

His attention was immediately diverted by a dissertation on the 'science of vampires':

Vampires appear to be immune to diseases like cancer. It is possible that they possess telomerase in their cells, protecting them from senescence. Thus, if at the molecular level, a vampire's body can produce the conditions that (1) make the cells divide indefinitely but remain immune to disease, or (2) stop them from dividing altogether without death setting in, then the genetic damage involved in aging is irrelevant: it doesn't occur.

Another:

Vampires thrive on blood, thus acquiring a double-edged allure. They hold the threat of stealing our most precious substance, but through that same substance may also deliver ecstasy and transformation.

The shaman had already slipped back downstairs and left Ramonne to his reading.

After a marathon absorption of vampire 'facts' and lore, some of which Ramonne had already learned through trial and error, he acknowledged the following about his kind:

Dracula, though wonderful folklore, is nonsense. Garlic. Mirrors. Stakes through the heart. Crosses. All nonsense.

Vampires know nothing of God.

Dark angels have always walked the earth looking for souls to steal.

They can survive by drinking animal blood—snakes are best —but just barely.

The Dark Gift is different for each vampire. Some can read thoughts. Some can project thoughts. Some can do both.

They get stronger day by day, night by night. Vampires love beauty. They feed on it.

They can move swiftly, without causing a stir, among mortals.

Sleep can be had without a coffin, but sleeping the day in a coffin resuscitates and strengthens the vampire.

Vampires grow stronger with time. The ancient ones are the strongest.

Sunlight alone can kill the young—seventy years or less; mortal age does not count.

They can also be extinguished by falling on a fire—'suicide'—if they choose. But they lose that ability to 'seek oblivion' the older and more powerful they get.

One can only kill the older forsaken on hallowed ground. First decapitation, and then destruction of the corpse by sunlight.

———

"Did you find what you were seeking?"

Ramonne was startled by the shaman's voice. He had forgotten the little man completely. He closed the Hodder book and put it gently back on the shelf. He looked outside. It was still dark, but he needed to get moving.

"Very interesting. Thank you."

"My pleasure." The white eyeballs sparkled as the shaman smiled.

"I fear there are some pages missing," Ramonne said. "Specifically SPELLS, CURSES, AND TALISMANS."

"Ahh. Well, the books are very old, I'm afraid."

Ramonne studied the man a moment. He was lying. This he knew, in spite of his having trouble reading his thoughts. The shaman was somehow able to put up a mental barrier of some sort.

Very curious.

"There is other knowledge you possess that is of interest to me, as well," Ramonne said.

"Anything. I am your servant."

"You gave two amulets to Khun Kanchana. What is their origin?"

"Filipino. They were made from silver bullets used to keep the *manananggal* at bay. This vampire is known for a tongue so long it is said it can suck a baby right out of a pregnant woman's womb, while she sleeps. I performed a powerful incantation over them as an added precaution."

"Are there any more of these...amulets?"

Charoen smiled as he pulled on a leather cord about his neck. "Just this one." The silver talisman slid out from his blouse and reflected the candle's flickering light.

Reflexively, Ramonne hissed.

"I see it works," the shaman bravely offered.

"You have no need for it, my friend," Ramonne declared.

"Perhaps. All the same, I think I shall continue to wear it."

"As you wish." *Save your puny life...for a while.* "May I borrow the books?"

"Please. They're yours. A gift."

"Thank you. You are most kind."

"Not at all. It is I who should thank you. Your regeneration was a great success for me. Very positive. Your powers humble me."

"I'm not sure what to say about that. As I told Khun Kanchana, it was not *my* idea to come back. I had no choice."

"The lady had a choice." Charoen smiled again. Ramonne was becoming very annoyed with the little blind man's smile. "She'd rather be damned than die."

Enough. This man's time was running out.

Ramonne placed the books in a leather satchel and hoisted it to his shoulder.

"Where will you go, now that you've left Khun Kanchana?"

Ramonne turned on the man, his yellow eyes aglow. *How does he know this? Can this mortal actually read minds? Does he possess the gift for real?*

Charoen smiled his Cheshire cat grin.

Very dangerous. Too dangerous to live.

Ramonne approached and reached out for the man's throat. But something stayed his hand. A force kept him from squeezing the life out of the little gnome.

He retreated.

He re-shouldered the bag and left.

The man continued to smile and stare into the void.

Soon, Ramonne vowed.

———

"Khun Larue. Good of you to come. Please, have a seat."

Lieutenant-Colonel Samarat escorted Martin into his utilitarian corner office and shut the door.

Martin felt a chill. This had been Boonsong's office. This was where he'd met with Martin and Jonathan, the vampire hunter, before the aborted rescue of Boonsong's daughter that cost Jonathan his life.

But destroyed the vampire.

Or so he thought.

"Coffee?"

"No thank you. Water will be fine."

Martin was feeling parched.

"Of course." Samarat pushed a button on his intercom and spoke to the voice on the other end.

"Khun Larue, my English is not so good. May we speak in Thai?"

"*Khrap*," Martin acknowledged.

"Good. I heard you were fluent. How many years have you been here?"

"Fifteen. And let's cut the bullshit, Lieutenant-Colonel. You know exactly how long I've been here. You know where I was born, my bank account balance…hell, you probably know the last time I took a shit."

Samarat leaned back in his chair. "Strong language for a monk."

"I'm not a monk. I *was* a novice. I studied the meditative arts. It was a form of therapy."

"Why would you need 'therapy,' Khun Larue? Seems to me that a multi-million-dollar inheritance ought to lead one to a fairly stress-free existence."

"One would think so. Unfortunately, that is not the case. Again…I'm sure you're well aware of this."

The lieutenant-colonel leafed through some papers while a young uniformed cop put a glass of water in front of Martin and a small, very dark coffee in front of Samarat. The colonel dismissed him and he snapped a salute and left the room.

"All right Khun Larue. Let's cut the 'bullshit' as you say." He slid an official looking document across the desk to Martin.

"What is this?"

"Read it. You do *read* Thai, don't you?"

Martin did. He picked it up. It was an immigration document.

"I'm being *deported*?"

"You have no visa, Khun Larue."

Americans were allowed to stay in Thailand for just thirty days without a visa. To stay longer, various visas were available, but none longer than ninety days. Martin, the rich eccentric, was in the habit of simply getting on a plane every thirty days. He'd been doing that for fifteen years. It wasn't until he met Ramonne that he had ever bothered to get a visa.

"I've been in a monastery for a year."

"And while you were in the monastic environment, you were granted special dispensation. But that was only so long as you wore the robes."

Martin thought about this. "All right, I'll leave. I'll get a visa and return."

"I'm afraid that may be difficult. You've been classified as… how can I put this delicately…'undesirable.'"

"What?" Martin grabbed up the document and studied it further.

"*Terrorist*. It says 'terrorist.'"

Samarat smiled. "I was being polite."

"Don't. It doesn't suit you."

Samarat merely shrugged. Martin slid the paper back to him.

"What do you want?"

The lieutenant-colonel had a file-folder on his desk. He opened it. On the top was a picture of a beautiful young lady. This too, came across the stainless-steel desk to Martin.

"Areeya Boonsong. She also seems to have suffered from stress."

Areeya? Martin knew her by her nickname, Yaya.

"Well, that's understandable. She lost her father."

"Her father and you were not exactly friends, were you?"

"Hardly. He had me arrested for murder." Martin shuddered when he recalled that the stinking jail where he'd spent the very worst week of his life was right under their feet.

"And he also cleared you of the charges."

"I was innocent."

"Yes. Of course. Back to the girl. Have you seen her since… since that night?"

"No. Why?"

"Just curious. She also went looking for therapy. Hers was a little different. She ended up in Sritanya Hospital."

Martin recognized the name of Bangkok's infamous mental institute. In a country of limited public services, a government mental facility was one of the last places Martin would have imagined the young society girl would have gone.

"How did she end up there?"

"You remember Pee Lokmon. The club owner and her fiancé?"

Martin did. He and Jonathan Peyton had followed Yaya to Pee's club in their hunt for Ramonne. It was in the club that Ramonne kidnapped her in a spectacular one-sided battle.

"Apparently she was out of her mind with crazy tales of *phii dibs* drinking blood, sleeping in coffins, and general hysteria."

And I wondered whether he would believe me.

"Khun Pee said he had no choice," Samarat added.

"Where is she now?"

"She's back at her father's house. The wedding is off." The colonel returned to the folder. He had another picture. This was a passport photo of Jonathan Peyton. The blond-haired man looked so relaxed and happy. Martin tried to put the image he'd always carry with him out of his head. The image of Jonathan— his spine shattered by a 200-foot fall—pleading with his red-rimmed, undead eyes, pleading with Martin to kill him.

And Martin racking the shotgun one more time and granting the request.

"This man, Jonathan Peyton. He was a friend of yours, wasn't he?"

"Yes."

"And he also fell into the river and drowned that night at Wat Arun—during the struggle with the kidnapper—yes?"

Martin hesitated.

"Yes."

"Khun Larue. Two men drowned that night. The kidnapper —an unidentified *farang*—and Mr. Peyton. Both bodies were never recovered. Only Colonel Boonsong's body was found. He had suffered massive throat lacerations, leaving his body virtually empty of blood."

Samarat went back to the file again. There, slightly yellow with more than a year's aging, was the *Bangkok Times* article that had started it all:

BANGRAK SERIAL KILLER.

The mutilated bodies of five young women between the ages of 17 and 22 are known to have been discovered in the Hernando Cemetery on Silom Road between November 25th, 1992 and last Friday. Rather than investigating these grizzly murders directly, the Bangrak police are suspected of being involved in a cover-up, going so far as to actually falsify the causes of death and location of the discovery of the girls' bodies.

"I have read your article, Khun Larue. I had it translated."

Martin cringed. He really wasn't ready to return to the cell in the basement, where he had spent the worst week of his life.

Next came the photos. Five girls, over a ten-year period. Each splayed naked atop a tomb in Hernando Cemetery on Silom Road.

Good Lord. Martin choked back tears. It had been a long time since he'd seen them.

"It wasn't hard to find these, Martin. In fact, the *Bangkok Times'* managing director was eager to show them to me. I had the unique distinction of being the first law enforcement officer to inquire into their existence."

The ceiling seemed to get a little closer to Martin's head. The tiles on the floor were starting to swim.

"Khun Larue, I know about these girls. I know about

Colonel Boonsong. I also know that when human arteries are severed, as in each case, the pressure of the flowing blood is such that there should be blood everywhere—within a ten to thirty-foot radius. And yet, in each case, the amount of spilled blood was minimal. Barely a few drops."

He threw two more photos on to the pile. These were full color.

Johnny Boy. Gunshot to the head. Lying on the floor of his white-on-white penthouse.

Rak. Driver for Interior Vice Minister Surapol. His throat also ripped to shreds.

"Khun Larue. These two events happened over the New Year holiday, this year, barely two weeks ago.

"In this instance—" He held up Rak's photo. "Five armed men were killed. This man was also drained of his blood. And Interior Minister Surapol—" He produced another photo.

Oh God. Just like 'headless Hans.' Hans had been Martin's 'bodyguard' after the newspaper article was published, and the first of the vampire's victims that Martin knew personally.

The vice minister's body lay slumped in the rear of his limo. His head was missing.

"A tall, well-built *farang* was described as the perpetrator in this instance. He was said to be impervious to their weapons. Bullets, apparently, passed right through him."

Samarat closed the file and leaned in close to Martin. "Khun Larue, I know that what you wrote about was true. I don't know the details—they died with Lieutenant-Colonel Boonsong—but I can tell you this: I am a different type of police officer. I am an *honest* cop. I don't take bribes."

Martin picked up the immigration document.

"*Terrorist*? That doesn't seem too honest to me."

Samarat smiled. "I didn't say the law couldn't be bent sometimes to get results."

"What do you want from me."

"Just the truth, Khun Larue. Just the truth."

7

It began with a waitress. Many things do. Good meals, good times.

She was extraordinarily pretty, with wild, curly, gypsy hair. It was the hair that first caught Ramonne's eye.

He was at Ban Klang Nam, a favorite haunt. It was a few kilometers south of the Oriental Hotel and a whole world away. It was mainly a local crowd, the ambience being that of a relative's large old rambling house by the river.

It was inexpensive, and Ramonne was still operating on a small stipend he'd received from Kanchana. It was to have been a weekly allowance, but Ramonne had only lasted a week with the she-devil. He wasn't desperate...*yet*. He had found a godown near the paper mill just past the Port Authority. Loh had negotiated the lease and paid a year in advance, on the condition of complete privacy. It took half of Ramonne's total worldly funds, but he was away from the she-devil and had a home for his modest possessions: two suits, two books, and a coffin.

Hardly his style. Things would have to change.

The price of food at the restaurant really didn't matter as Ramonne didn't eat; he drank. And the simple Bordeaux that he'd convinced the owner to buy ten years before, was still available, affordable, and very drinkable. He could easily go through two bottles at a sitting.

The other great benefit to Ramonne was the restaurant's proximity to the Klong Toey docks. This was a prime feeding ground for Ramonne. Drunken sailors come and go at all hours, and are seldom missed. Ramonne was planning on leaving the restaurant at closing, and figured he'd be 'dining' himself within the next hour after that.

As a waiter opened the second bottle, he studied the girl.

Ramonne had always liked waitresses. He liked the smell of cigarettes and grease in their hair and on their skin. It was a smell of *life*. Ramonne was a vampire and he was in the business of death, but he appreciated life. He admired those who lived life to the fullest. He despised those who wasted it.

This waitress had a regal manner about her. She threw her head back when she laughed—something she did quite regularly. He watched her move from table to table. She juggled the customers' drunken advances, their confusing orders, all with equanimity and good humor. Ramonne was impressed.

She also had a killer body. Ramonne was attracted. Perhaps tonight's sport would be something a little more exotic than a drunken sailor.

He started to fantasize about her—a trait he realized he still shared with mortal men. There's that time before you get to know a woman when you fantasize about her. You envision her, naked. You imagine the two of you together. You imagine what it will be like. What she'll be like.

And if it seems real, if you can almost taste it, then maybe… just maybe…it will become real.

At this point Ramonne took a giant step away from mortal men. Ramonne could *guarantee* that this woman and he would be together. Ramonne could guarantee that she would be his.

For Ramonne had the ability to control her mind.

The only thing he could not guarantee was that she would

make it through the night. That was most improbable and unfortunate.

This was Ramonne's one great shortcoming as the ultimate lover. Most women wanted to live to talk about it.

"Prichada!"

The young man didn't say the name politely. He snapped it.

She stopped dead in her tracks. She almost spilled a customer's beer. She apologized and hurried to the table the young man had just taken by the river's edge.

He took out a cigarette and waited for her to light it.

Arrogant little prick.

She produced matches, and, for the first time, Ramonne thought he detected a sense of nervousness about her.

The young man puffed on his cigarette while the girl just stood waiting. Finally he spoke and she bowed slightly and then backed away from him.

This wasn't the flirtatious, composed manner that she had exhibited with the other customers.

Who is this asshole?

Ramonne was also seated at a table by the riverside. His ability to read men's thoughts was limited by the same physical restriction as his ability to hear their spoken voice.

He was just out of earshot.

Prichada brought the insolent young man a bottle of Jack Daniel's and an ice bucket. She dutifully filled his glass with equal amounts of bourbon and water.

She placed a menu down on the table and backed away. The young man continued to smoke without looking at the menu.

Finally he stubbed out the cigarette and picked up the menu. A thin manila envelope was beneath it. He set the menu aside.

The young man made sure his back was to the water before opening the envelope and glancing at the contents. Ramonne caught a glimpse of two photographs, a handwritten note, and what appeared to be a map.

He returned the material to the envelope and went back to his drink. And another cigarette.

The girl never returned to the table. After a few minutes, he drained his glass and screwed the top back on the bottle. He laid a couple of 500-baht notes under the glass, stuffed the envelope into his back pocket as he stood up, and flicked the cigarette into the river.

He walked directly toward Ramonne as he headed for the exit.

Pure evil.

That was the first thought that Ramonne tuned into as the young man walked by him. Their eyes met, just briefly.

Without a word being exchanged, Ramonne felt a challenge.

This arrogant, evil young man fancies himself my equal.

Now Ramonne was really intrigued, and decided to follow him, determined to find out who he was.

And then probably destroy him.

The waitress would have to wait.

———

The wind was refreshing. It was unseasonably warm in Bangkok for January, and the occasional breezes that blew through the four-story gap on the Banyan Tree Hotel were a welcome relief.

The hotel had opened under a different banner just before the economy went down the toilet in 1997. Ramonne's general distaste for the modern world did not automatically preclude those buildings whose architects managed to embellish the landscape rather than degrade it with one disgrace after another. He admired the slim silhouette of the skyscraper, whose dominant feature was the gaping hole that began on the fifty-first floor. Here, an open-air atrium hosted a small exercise pool, a Jacuzzi, and a full-size banyan tree. The exposure to the elements, the view, the entire feeling was spectacular, and

Ramonne had used it as a leaping off point, literally, to some of his finer meals. He'd spot an open window somewhere below or above, and climb up or down to it.

Tonight, he was a fly on the wall again. He stood just outside the glass railing that prevented the guests being swept off the deck, pressed into a corner, observing.

The young man—Somchai, or Nit as he was known—had proven to be a curiosity to Ramonne, and this was the second night that he had occupied his time.

The first night, Ramonne had followed Nit to a familiar nightclub on Bangkok's infamous Royal City Avenue. Outside the Sound & Light Club, Ramonne watched as Nit secured *yaa baa*, or 'crazy drug' as the powerful amphetamine was literally known.

This one was totally worthless. Ramonne had almost dismissed the man and devoured him on the spot, when he saw him unlock a silver Mercedes parked in the disco's lot.

Curious. He had taken a taxi from the restaurant. Why? When he had a car? Why? Unless he was covering his tracks.

Ramonne had kept his own taxi, and he motioned for the driver to follow the Mercedes.

Nit pulled into a parking ramp at the CP Tower on Silom Road, opposite Patpong. Ramonne knew that the building was all offices and that some residents of the area paid to park their cars there. He paid the cab fare and waited on the steps outside McDonald's for the young man to emerge.

Within ten minutes the man walked out the side entrance to the building and crossed the busy street. He went down the alley that was in fact the entry to Patpong 2. Just past the Caffè di Roma, where Ramonne had spent many hours with a fine bottle of red watching the passing parade of hookers, choosing his victim for the night, Nit slipped a key into a locked door at the rear of a seedy bar.

Ramonne stopped and looked up. A rusty fire escape clung to the exterior of the six-story building. Laundry hung outside most of the windows. The lights were out in nearly all of the shotgun-style apartments. He waited and watched. Soon a light went on in an apartment on the top floor. Ramonne leaped up and caught the bottom of the second-floor fire escape. He swung himself up and onto the landing.

Outside the man's window, Ramonne watched as he mixed the speed with another powder, this one slightly brown in shade. He cooked the mixture over a small lighter and injected it into his tied-off arm.

Nit slipped into a haze, and Ramonne slipped into his apartment.

Ramonne could easily move undetected among mortals; among stoned, nodding-off mortals he could be a bull elephant and still move about unseen.

The first thing Ramonne looked at was the envelope. It was on the 'kitchen' table. He opened it. The picture was of a middle-aged man he'd seen in the papers. Retired army general Posit Thansarong had had a very tawdry public affair with the young wife of the owner of one of the kingdom's largest department store chains. When the shopping tycoon confronted the general and produced a series of incriminating photos of the general and the wife and demanded an end to the affair, the general had apparently torn up the photos and slapped and kicked the businessman until he was taken to Bumrungrad Hospital for treatment. While in hospital, two of the prestigious chain stores burned to the ground, the fire department apparently helpless to put out the blazes; some said they stood by and let the buildings burn, causing billions of baht in uninsured damage.

The general's name was written in neat block letters under the photos.

The map was a Xerox of the floor plan of the fifty-first floor of the Banyan Tree Hotel, the open-air pool and spa adjacent to the health club. On it was written tomorrow's date and the time: 9:30 p.m.

One more piece of paper merely had the figure 1,000,000 baht written on it. Twenty five thousand US dollars. Ramonne emitted a low whistle.

"Huh?" Nit had stirred and almost opened his eyes.

Ramonne ignored him and replaced the envelope. He continued to inspect the apartment. It was basically one long room. A half-wall divided an area with a bed from the living area. Except for its general untidiness, it wasn't a bad place. Ramonne could imagine living here, right *in* Patpong, one of his favorite feeding grounds. Its misplaced denizens—prostitutes, drug-addicts, and drunks—were easy targets and, like the sailors, hardly missed in the harsh light of day. He used to have an arrangement with the police to cover up his tracks. They'd take the bodies he'd conveniently deposit in Hernando Cemetery and turn them into suicides, hit and run victims, drownings, whatever. For this he paid a modest fee. Modest until that prick Boonsong had begun bleeding him dry. It was a metaphor Ramonne had used before, and every time he did, he had to chuckle.

Again, the stoned man stirred.

Ramonne moved into the bedroom and opened the closet. A locked gun cabinet occupied one side. He slowly turned the dial. Hands that could read Braille without a lesson had no problem with a simple combination lock. In seconds it was open.

He whistled again. Nit had been a very bad boy.

A .30-caliber rifle with a night scope was in the corner. Next to it was a Browning 12-gauge pump shotgun, two 357 Smith & Wessons, one with a specially fitted silencer, a .22 rifle, also with an infrared scope, stun guns, tasers, boxes of ammunition, a box of latex surgical gloves, wigs, ID badges, eyeglass frames with clear lenses, smoke bombs, and a small but very complete tool box. A briefcase was also locked. Ramonne spun the dials and opened it. Stacks of 1,000-baht notes and a year-old copy of *Playboy*. Probably four million baht, Ramonne estimated.

Ramonne had contemplated taking the money. But he closed the case and put it back.

Later.

He shut and locked the gun case.

As he stepped back through the window onto the fire escape, he studied the blissed-out zombie on the couch.

One more night. Ramonne would allow his curiosity to run its course.

Realizing he was hungry, he ignored the fire escape and dropped silently six floors to the street below.

———

Tonight, Ramonne arrived early at the Banyan Tree Hotel. Getting to the fifty-first floor was tricky, as the elevators didn't stop there. One had to enter through the spa on the fifty-third. The open atrium was reserved for health spa guests only.

Ramonne willed the desk attendant not to see him, and he entered the spa unnoticed.

General Thansarong was on a massage table. A hole in the table held his head, and he faced down to a bowl of floating flowers. Aromatherapy candles burned as the masseuse kneaded his massive shoulders. The general had already drifted into a fog.

Incongruous to the tranquility of the spa, a stern-faced bodyguard sat in a chair opposite and stared stoically ahead.

Dying for a cigarette.

Ramonne picked up the thought.

Now that he was in the spa, Ramonne didn't bother to disguise his movements, and simply passed by the open massage room without a word.

As he stepped into the four-story hole on the fifty-first floor and felt the delicious night breeze, he noticed he wasn't the only one who was early. A young man with orange spiky hair was busy trimming the banyan tree with a pair of shears.

He wore a blue jumpsuit and worked slowly, quietly, patiently.

Nit. Ramonne observed. He willed the young man not to see him.

At precisely 9:30 p.m. the general entered the atrium. He wore a huge white, terrycloth robe. He was accompanied by a spa attendant, who led him to the hot tub.

Ramonne was already tucked into a corner of the building, outside the glass rail, perched on the ledge. Chong, the bodyguard, came down the stairs alone. He reached in his pocket and produced a packet of Krong Thip. Glad to be outside and able to smoke, he moved to the railing and lit up. He was inches from Ramonne.

The attendant removed the general's robe and held his arm as he walked into the bubbling waters. Once he was settled, she bowed and backed gracefully away. She returned to the health spa.

Now it was just the general in the tub and the bodyguard at the rail.

The orange-haired Nit the tree hairdresser was no longer trimming the banyan, but was now operating an electric floor polisher. It hummed monotonously as he moved it over the smooth marble surface.

The bodyguard puffed silently on his cigarette as he enjoyed the view. The night was crystal clear and you could see for miles—to the docks at Klong Toey, the ships anchored in the bend of the river, to the sleek span of the Rama IX Bridge. As he blew out the smoke, it wafted right into Ramonne.

A smoking ban imposed throughout the kingdom, and this idiot blows smoke in my face without realizing it? He was moments away from flinging the fool off the building, but instead held his breath.

The general leaned his head back and allowed the water to totally engulf him. Nit the floor polisher moved the machine slowly across the stones.

The 220-volt, 1,000-amp motor hummed louder and louder as it got closer to the contented army general.

Ahh. Not a bad plan for such a young man. An accident kills the general; unidentified maintenance man flees the scene.

Ramonne smiled to himself. But then he realized the flaw.

What about the bodyguard?

Then he realized that Nit hadn't seen Chong. He was so focused on the general that he'd never noticed the bodyguard.

Nit was a mere yard away, when the General slowly opened his eyes.

"Hey you. Boy! Get away from here."

As the general bellowed, his bodyguard turned. Then three things happened.

Nit moved forward with the machine.

Chong reached for his gun.

Ramonne grabbed the bodyguard and flung him into space.

Nit paused at the sound and turned to the railing.

Nothing.

He turned back and pushed the floor polisher into the Jacuzzi. The general snapped and stiffened. His eyes bulged as 220 volts coursed through his body.

Without a backward glance, Nit calmly walked to the exit.

8

The buzzer said simply "Boonsong." Martin hesitated and then pressed it. A soft chime sounded in the distance.

After a few minutes, the stained-glass door was opened and a young woman stood behind the locked screen.

"Yes?"

"Khun Areeya?" He knew it was her. The hair was longer, a line or two around the eyes, but she was still the graceful young beauty he had watched Ramonne throw over his shoulder and leap through a plate-glass window as he kidnapped her from a crowded nightclub. "I knew your father."

"I know who you are." Apparently she recognized him, too. "Please go away." She started to shut the door.

"Please. We need to talk."

"No we don't. We need to forget." "Areeya. Your father's killer is alive."

There. He'd said it. Now maybe he could force himself to believe it.

They sat in a comfortable little parlor. A Buddhist shrine to her father held a prominent place on one wall. Small colored lights were arranged around several offering plates and incense holders. A framed black and white photograph of the lieutenant-colonel stood in the center. On the opposite wall were his certificates, diplomas, humanitarian awards, etcetera.

"I thought you destroyed the beast. I thought that was your job. I thought that was why you were there."

Martin nodded. "Yes. I thought I did destroy the 'beast' as you called him. I saw him wither to dust and ash in the morning. Yet, someone or something has managed to bring him back…and he's carrying on his gruesome work."

"How is that possible?"

"How was it possible for him to exist in the first place? What *fallen angel* offended the Lord so that he was cursed in such a way? Where on the eternal wheel of life, death, and reincarnation did it begin? These are questions I sought answers to and have finally given up on. Now I just accept that he existed."

"I can't." She looked at her father's photograph. "Do you know the hell I've been through?"

Martin nodded. "I was told. I'm sorry."

"Do you think I *wanted* to be incarcerated in that house of horrors?"

"No. No I don't." Martin tried to look the girl in the eye, but she stared into space, keeping her distance. "It was involuntary, I take it."

"*Yes* it was involuntary. That oaf I was supposed to marry had his goons take me there kicking and screaming. It was my second kidnapping in as many months." Now she looked him in the eye.

Hers were wet.

"What do you want from me?"

"You know who he is. *What* he is. You can help."

"They gave me shock treatment. *Shock treatment*. To make me forget."

"My Lord. I had no idea."

"No one does.

"Seeing my father in the hands of that monster, spending the night with him in his lair, watching him sleep in a coffin…I thought I had been to hell. I had no idea that my descent had just begun. It was when I was dragged through the doors of Sritanya that I truly was doomed."

"But you're here now. You're free. How did you manage that?"

"How does anyone get out of a looney bin? They *cured* me. I shut up. I quit talking about vampires. I played the game. I got smart. Now do you understand why I can't help you?"

"Areeya, you and I both know him. We can identify him if he truly exists again."

"Dozens of people saw him at the club. You were shooting at him as I recall."

"Pee convinced the press, with police collaboration, that it was just a publicity stunt. Nobody knows the truth."

"So that's what he was up to while I was getting electric brain massages. The prick. Must have thought the 'truth' would be bad for business."

"I doubt if he knew the truth, Areeya. That's what I'm trying to tell you. We're the only two alive who know what really happened."

"Fuck you."

"Please."

"I mean it. Fuck you. How dare you come to me and expect me to plunge myself back into that nightmare again? Give me one reason?" If she'd been closer to him, she would have slapped him. Martin could feel it.

"Do you know what the only positive thing is that came out of this…this—"

Even now she had no words to adequately describe what she'd been through. What *they'd* been through. Instead she just sighed.

"What?" Martin wanted to know.

"I'm sober. Clean. Drug free."

"That's good."

"No. It sucks. I hate my life. I'm bored out of my fucking mind."

"Maybe there's your reason."

"What?"

"To help me."

"Because I'm bored?"

"To keep you straight."

"Do you know what you're saying?"

"Yes. I think so."

"Mr. Larue. That is your name, isn't it? Martin Larue?"

"Yes. But please, call me Martin."

"Martin. I'd wake up and have a snort of cocaine before I'd have a cup of coffee. And that was on a weekday. By six o'clock I'd finished a bottle of vodka and was switching to champagne. Do you know the golden rule of drinking?"

"No."

"Booze then beer, never fear. Wine then liquor, never sicker. I learned that by the time I was sixteen.

"Two or three grams of cocaine, a bottle of vodka, two bottles of champagne, hashish if available, grass if not, and a couple of valiums to help me get a few hours sleep. Next day, I'd do it all over again. I'm 22, Martin. It didn't kill me...but given a little more time, I'm sure it would. And you know what?"

"What?"

"I feel like getting high right now."

"Of course you do. That's the nature of the disease."

"How the fuck would you know?"

"I watched my brother go through exactly what you described. The only difference was, he didn't stop. It *did* kill him. I couldn't...I *didn't* help him. Maybe I can help you."

"I've stayed in this fucking house for four months now. I

can't call my friends. You know why?"

"Yes. They'll just want you to get high. You need new friends."

He thought about this.

"And so do I."

They sat in silence. A minute passed.

"What did you do?" She asked.

"What do you mean?"

"After it was over. What did you do?"

"I went into a monastery."

"Did it work?"

"I thought so, yes."

"But?"

"But now I don't know. Now I'm like you. I wanted it to be over. To be the past. To be forgotten."

"But?"

"But this policeman. Lieutenant-Colonel—"

"Samarat."

"Yes. Samarat. He came to see me."

"He came to see me, also. I didn't let *him* in the door."

"I did. He showed me photos. He told me things. He made me believe."

"What did you tell him?"

"Everything."

"Did he believe you?"

"I have no idea. The important thing is, I believed him. He convinced me that Ramonne is back."

"How is that possible?"

"I don't know. But I do know that a country that can regularly turn big-footed, clumsy, upcountry male bumpkins into gorgeous young anatomically correct Japanese girls, can probably figure out how to regenerate the living dead."

She laughed. It was the first time he'd heard her laugh. He liked it. It suited her.

"That's better. You should do that more often."

"What?"

"Laugh."

She smiled. Another quality that had been lacking until now.

"I wish I could."

"I'll help with that, also."

"Really?" She looked at him. Really looked at him; perhaps for the first time.

"Let's see. You'll keep me straight. Keep me sober. Make me laugh…And the price for all of this service?"

"Help me. Help me find him. Help me destroy him."

———

"One million baht. Count it, if you like."

The money was in a briefcase, in 1,000-baht notes, neatly wrapped and stacked.

Nit smiled and closed the case. "I won't insult you Jao Phor. I know it is all there."

The man Nit referred to as *Jao Phor* or 'Godfather,' Ping Narong, was well-dressed, well groomed, Chinese, and in his mid fifties. He had a no-nonsense air about him, as did the three men in matching black safari suits who attended him.

The clandestine meeting was held in a back room of a snooker hall owned by Ping. Cases of Singha beer and Mekong whiskey, stacked to the ceiling, filled most of the room. The godfather sat behind a metal table, his back to a breeze-block wall. One of his men stood by the only entrance to the room—a metal door with a big sliding bolt. The other two stood on either side of Ping. A double-tubed fluorescent light hung low over the table casting the only light.

Ping smiled and nodded at Nit.

Nit did a deep and reverential *wai* to the godfather, picked up the case, and left the room.

———

Nit stopped at the mouth of the alley. He lit a cigarette, took a drag, and then pressed the button on his car keys. His silver Mercedes chirped twice and blinked its lights. He had his hand on the door handle when—

"Half of that is mine."

"What?"

Nit spun around.

Ramonne stood in the alley, casually leaning against a brick wall.

"Who the fuck are you?"

"Your savior."

"*Savior*? What the fuck are you talking about?" He started to reach into his pocket.

"Don't." Ramonne's tone was like ice.

Nit let the pistol slide back into his pocket and Ramonne was suddenly an inch from his face. Nit never saw him move.

Ramonne sniffed like a wolf.

"What *is* your problem, man?" Nit wanted to push him away, but something made him think twice.

"Like I said…half your money."

"Man, you really are flipped. Why would I give you half of anything?"

"Because I earned it. Think back, Nit. To last night."

Nit was startled by the mention of his name.

"You were about to electrocute the good general—"

"I don't know what you're talking about." Nit decided enough was enough. "Fuck you." He flung his cigarette at Ramonne. Sparks flew as it bounced off Ramonne's silk suit. Nit opened the car door.

Ramonne slammed it on his hand.

"*Aiieee!*"

"You young are so impatient. Just shut up and listen."

Ramonne kept the door closed on his hand, pinning him. Nit grimaced in pain but remained silent.

"As I said, you were about to electrocute the general when he yelled at you. At that moment his bodyguard pulled his gun."

"And fell over the rail."

"You think you're that lucky? This is what I'm talking about. Here you are, red assassin—well paid I might add—and yet you failed to note a six-foot professional security guard. You never saw him, Nit. I know. I was there."

"Where the fuck were you?"

"Outside the rail, watching."

"Bullshit. That's fifty stories. Nobody would go out on that ledge."

"You're only alive because I *was* on that ledge. *I* pulled the bodyguard over the rail."

Nit looked into the yellow eyes.

He thought about what the stranger had just said.

"That's the stupidest story I ever heard."

Ramonne relaxed his grip on the door and Nit pulled his hand free. "Last chance. Half the money."

Nit drew his pistol.

Ramonne smiled. "Then I'll take it all." And sank his teeth into the man's throat while twisting the gun away. It fired, twice, and then dropped to the pavement.

A few long minutes passed and then the body stopped twitching.

Ramonne let the boy fall, taking the briefcase from him as he did.

He thought for a moment, and then decided to gamble.
What the hell.
He was a vampire. What did he have to lose?

———

"Jao Phor. This crazy *farang* has Nit's money. Says he wants to give it back."

Clearly annoyed, Ping looked up and snarled, "What?"

"Nit. He didn't earn the money. He was sloppy. Therefore I'm returning it to you."

Ramonne had Lek, the man from the front door, in a vise-grip about his neck. In his other hand he had the briefcase. He dropped the case on the table and released Lek. Lek immediately drew a pistol. Two other guns were already leveled at Ramonne. He ignored them and opened the case.

"It's all there. Untouched."

Ping, now unfazed, turned to Lek. "Count it."

Lek hesitated, his finger itching to pull the trigger.

"I said count it."

Lek reluctantly put down his gun and moved toward the money.

"Where is Nit?"

"Unfortunately he is no longer with us."

"Nit is dead?"

Ramonne nodded.

The godfather fixed the intruder in his steely glare.

"You?"

Ramonne nodded again.

The fingers on the other two guns twitched and tightened.

Ping began to laugh. His raucous laughter was contagious, and the other men began to laugh, also.

Laugh at Ramonne.

Ramonne remained stoical, but made a silent vow.

"You expect me to believe a pansy like you killed Nit? That's preposterous. Why?

"Nit was sloppy. He would have been killed last night and failed in his mission if I had not intervened."

"Oh? How is that?"

"The general had a bodyguard. Nit never saw him. He would have shot Nit if I hadn't thrown him off the building."

"You say you were there?"

"I was."

"Since you'll never leave the room alive, I'll humor you…I questioned Nit about the bodyguard's death. Obviously we would have preferred for it to seem that the general was killed accidentally. However, Nit assured us there was no other way. He said he threw the bodyguard over the rail and then killed the general."

"Nit lied."

The godfather pondered this

Lek finished counting the money.

"It's all there."

Ping studied Ramonne for another moment and then he spoke.

"I think you're a cop and you're not on my payroll."

"If I was a cop, the money would not all be there. I have returned your money out of respect. Nit failed you. I thought you should know."

Another tense moment while Ping thought this over. He took out a cigar and reached for a match.

"Bullshit. You're a cop."

He struck the match.

"Kill him."

Ramonne moved without being seen. In an instant he pulled Lek in front of him, and Lek was immediately riddled with bullets.

When the men realized what had happened they stopped firing.

Ramonne tossed the dead man aside and grabbed the nearest pistol—still in its owner's grip—by its smoking barrel. He pulled it toward his chest.

The gunman smiled and fired. Twice.

Ramonne pushed the gun away and opened his shirt. There were two holes in his chest.

But no blood.

Now Ramonne smiled. He turned the barrel of the gun to the man's chest. The man's finger was frozen on the trigger. Ramonne looked deep into his eyes. He nodded.

Then the man shot himself and collapsed to the floor.

"*Fuck me!*" Ping still had the lit match in his hand. It burned his finger and he dropped it.

There was still one gun, admittedly a very shaky gun, pointed at Ramonne.

Ping waved his hand and the gun was holstered. The man stared open-mouthed at the two bodies before him.

Ping regained his composure and lit another match. He puffed on his cigar before speaking.

"Okay. You're not a cop. What *are* you?"

"Some call me undead. You Thais mistakenly call me *phii dib*. All you need to know is that I'm eternally damned. That makes me *very* dangerous."

"What do you want?"

Ramonne smiled and buttoned up his shirt. He put a finger though one of the bullet holes in his jacket.

"For one thing…a new suit."

"And a job."

———

Ramonne Delacroix became a hit man. Some would say he always was—but now he would be paid for it.

Ping Narong's hand was everywhere. Gambling, prostitution, drugs, arms trading, oil smuggling, stolen gems, poaching, logging, endangered species. If it was illegal, he was involved.

He rigged elections. He secured lucrative contracts for big businesses, and he bribed government officials to obtain prime land deals.

He even ran legitimate, though admittedly shady businesses: Nightclubs, go-go bars, and snooker halls.

He was the man to contact when you needed something fixed.

Or broken.

Ramonne soon proved invaluable.

9

———

"An inconvenience." That's what they called it.

A dozen men in crew cuts and tight uniforms marched into the bar and told the owner to turn off the music and turn on the lights. It wasn't enough that the law ordered the bars closed at one o'clock. Now, it seemed, they had to impose their physical presence upon the party revelers.

It had been a very long day and Denzel had looked forward to the night. He had planned his evening's events to allow him to arrive at the Q Bar at precisely 11:30. That was feeding time in this little zoo. The dance floor was packed with the prettiest girls in the kingdom. Models, actresses, secretaries, students, hookers—all gorgeous. Firm bums squeezed into leather microskirts and hip-hugging jeans, they gyrated to the non-stop trance mix with their arms over their heads and their noses turned up. Denzel floated among them like a dark bird of prey. His chocolate skin glowed in the black light, and beads of sweat shined on his corn-rowed hair.

He felt their eyes.

He knew their secret.

They would never admit it to their girlfriends, or anyone, but they desired him. They all wanted the black man. They all wanted to know if it was true. They wanted to get him alone. They wanted to explore his manhood. They wanted him to be bad to them.

They wanted *him*.

It never failed to amaze him, the utter wanton lust that was paid to a black man by the Asian woman. He'd first experienced it as a fullback at UCLA when his tight end, Lance Henderson, suggested they go to the Century Club in Century City. He had walked into a pulsating viper's nest of Japanese, Vietnamese, and Chinese vixens, tarted out to the nines and wantonly seducing every young black stud on the dance floor. Lance—his blond good looks usually guaranteeing that he never left a bar alone—was rejected, while jerry-curled Denzel was pounced upon, and ended up the night with his first multiple sex partner experience.

He signed with the Lions and went to Tokyo as a pro. He played two exhibition games in the Dome and never wanted to leave. The way the women lined up at his hotel to have sex with the black athletes, the way they offered him money—*offered him money*—for sex in nightclubs in Roppongi…it blew his mind.

He played ball until his knee gave out. After that, he used his celebrity to survive. At first it was endorsements—jeans, sneakers, junk food, and, in Japan, whiskey and cellphones. As he grew a bit longer in the tooth and less recognizable, these fell off.

And as his money waned, his overhead grew. He developed expensive habits. Drugs, mainly. As is the way of the world, he eventually became not just a user but a 'trader.' Denzel preferred that word over 'dealer.' Dealers were low life, petty hoods. Denzel had class. His face was still recognizable enough to get him through most American Customs checks with little more than a surprised look of recognition, followed by a request for an autograph.

Denzel Jefferson, former UCLA fullback and Detroit Lion, now international drug-trader, was in Bangkok to pick up ten kilos of pure heroin. He was to meet his connection at midnight in the Q Bar. Everything was perfect. Denzel would take the stash and a couple of little honeys back to his hotel and all would be cool.

But then the law showed up.

"The men will please line up on my right; the women to my left." The police sergeant said this twice. First in Thai. Then in perfect English.

Denzel watched in slack-jawed astonishment as the 200 or so party hearty clubbers begrudgingly did as was requested. A dozen cops had fanned out along the club's neon-tinged walls and sealed off the doors.

"The kingdom thanks you for your co-operation. We will get through this most efficiently if you all co-operate fully." The perfect English was starting to unravel. Denzel suspected that this was a rote speech, memorized phonetically for these occasions.

A young cop, his uniform as tight as the skin on a sausage, was distributing small plastic cups.

Shit. Denzel looked for an escape route, but there was none.

"We will be requesting your identity papers. Passports for foreigners please. And we will require a urine specimen please."

Urine sample. Denzel found himself mentally correcting the automaton. Exactly the last thing he wanted a cop to possess: a Dixie cup full of his tainted piss.

Fuck. What the hell happened to the Land of Smiles? Party-all-night, do-what-the-fuck-you-want Thailand?

Sweat rolled down his back. A cup was placed in his hand.

"The kingdom is plagued with drug dealers. 'Dealers of death' our prime minister has labeled them. Some of you may be their victims. To help us banish this scourge from our country and to render our official entertainment zones the purity they should possess, we must insist that you all be tested. If there are no traces of impurities you will be free to go.

If there are drugs detected, you will be sequestered. Thank you."

Impurities? Sequestered? Denzel exploded. He'd been snorting coke and Mexican brown for the last week. He'd actually brought drugs *to* Thailand. *Fuck. Fuck. Fuck.*

He fell in line on the right with the rest of the guys.

He was wedged between a Belgian banker—highly irate and already on his cellphone to his attorney—and a short British photographer who seemed to take it all in stride. As the unflattering glare of the 1,000-watt house lights in a room that was normally dark pointed out, it was the girls who were the most afraid of their circumstance. The men, mostly white foreigners, were upwardly mobile. They had money. But the girls—models, semi-models, students, pretty young things—most had no recourse. They had no fall-back plan—no attorneys, no bail money—should their piss turn up dirty.

They, like Denzel, were destined to be the victims of the night.

The others, the rich ones, would only have to answer to 'daddy.'

Denzel's wandering paranoia was jolted by the appearance of a pair of *yellow* eyes. "Mr. Jefferson?" They demanded.

"Yes?"

"Come with me."

The Bed Supper Club. White on white in white. Denzel was like a chocolate chip in a vanilla milkshake. How the man with the yellow eyes had gotten them past the cops at the door of the Q Bar, Denzel could not fathom. He assumed bribes had exchanged hands, because they appeared not to even *see* them as they boldly walked out the front.

'Bed' was just around the corner from the Q Bar, and Denzel followed the stranger without question. The tall man strode the *soi* at a brisk and determined pace. In one hand he carried a slim silver case.

My man. Denzel was impressed.

The exterior of the venue belied its interior. It looked to all the world like a huge section of drainage pipe, slightly compressed. A giant oval tube with stairs attached. Inside, however, the individual feel was diffused by an ambience of understated elegance. Beautiful young waitresses in white, loose-fitting cotton trousers and blouses seated guests on actual beds—hence the name—sheathed in white linen. Honeycombed alcoves ringed the oval interior. A disco adjoined the restaurant section and was the scene of most of the action at this late hour.

The yellow-eyed stranger was shown to an alcove and the waitress proffered a drinks menu. Before she could leave, he ordered a bottle of cabernet franc.

Denzel drew a deep breath and tried to act nonchalant. "So. How'd you do that?"

The stranger eyed him indifferently. "What?"

"You know. Get us past those five-o's. The pigs…You bribed 'em, right?"

He received no answer. He waited a full minute and gave up. Large white pillows invited Denzel to stretch out, and so he did. He put his hands behind his head.

The girl returned with the wine. She poured a small amount in a glass. The stranger sipped and smiled. She poured two full glasses, bowed and left them.

The stranger reached up and drew closed a white curtain. They were alone in a room of pure white. It was akin to being in a blizzard. With a *thunk* the stranger plopped his silver case on the table. He opened it. Inside were two double rows of small, fat bags of white powder.

Denzel smiled. He reached for the case, but the stranger snapped it shut. "Show me *yours.*" The yellow eyes glowed menacingly.

Denzel pulled his hand back and reached into his jacket

pocket. He watched for the flinch. He'd done this a hundred times or more, and every time he reached into his jacket pocket the other guy flinched. Expecting Denzel to pull out a rod. A gun. A deal-breaker. It was a natural reaction. It went with the territory.

He had learned to maintain eye contact—and to move *very* slowly. But this time there was no flinch. The stranger didn't move. He was rock steady. Unconcerned. He seemed like he could care less whether Denzel pulled out a wad of Benjamins or a 9-mm Berretta.

One cool fucking customer.

Denzel brought out a small black pouch.

The stranger's yellow eyes narrowed. "What is *that*?"

Denzel flashed his best toothpaste smile. He opened the pouch and extracted a dazzling amber gem the size of a small egg. "This is a Sienna opal. Street value: a quarter-million US. I was assured that your man would appreciate that we are offering you a considerable mark-up for your product by paying with a gem rather than cash."

Silence.

Denzel was pretty sure by now that silence was not a good thing with this man.

Without doubt, it made Denzel nervous. It was like the sound in his grandmother's house: The only thing you heard was the great clock on the mantel…ticking, ticking, ticking.

Except here there was no clock.

Finally the stranger leaned over the table. He took the gem in his hand and studied it. "Beautiful."

"Yeah," Denzel gladly chimed in. "One of a kind."

The stranger put the gem back in its pouch and slipped it into his coat pocket. "But this was not the deal."

He started to pull the briefcase off the table. Denzel slammed his hand down on it. "Fuck you." The stranger's eyes narrowed to slits, like a snake's.

Denzel kept his hand on the case. "You've got a gem that's

worth nearly twice your asking price. We're done. Give me the shit."

The stranger looked deep into Denzel's eyes. "Tell me. This idea of the gem being used instead of cash—were you privy to this exchange?"

Denzel paused. "I don't know what the fuck you're talking about." But as he said the words, the incident flashed through his mind. He had met his usual connection in front of the Regent Hotel. The holiday decorations had just been mounted, and a tree of lights illuminated the slick pompadour of the young Thai in the shark-skin suit. Johnny Boy Lao. He had handed Denzel a small black box. Puzzled, Denzel had opened it. Nestled inside in a velvet cocoon was the sparkling gem. The young man had whispered something in Denzel's ear and then walked down the marble staircase and got into a waiting car.

Snapping back to the present, Denzel locked eyes with the stranger. He knew that somehow the man had just witnessed his recollection of the meeting and exchange of the gem.

"He told me to exchange the gem for the drugs. No more cash. I thought you knew."

"The deal was cash. That is what I know. Therefore the deal is off."

The stranger pulled the case out from under Denzel's hand and off the table. He started to rise.

"Hey. Then give me back the motherfucking gem."

The stranger took the stone from his pocket. It sparkled in the light. He studied it and then put it back in his pocket. "Don't worry. I'll return it for you."

———

The waitress was reluctant to disturb the customers when the curtains were drawn. In a place known for intimacy and privacy, you could be shocked at what the customers got up to after a few drinks. Nat approached the alcove gingerly and waited outside a moment before drawing the curtain. She knew that her outline would be visible and they could expect her to come and take their dinner order. What she found when she opened the linen drape made her gasp for air.

She found herself gazing on a crimson tableaux. The white bed, cushions, and tablecloth were soaked in blood, and the young black man that she had been so attracted to when he arrived, had a gash across his throat that had nearly severed his head from his body.

She dropped her silver tray and screamed.

———

Ramonne's first professional assignment brought small-time hood Johnny Boy Lao to an early demise and secured a half million dollars in emeralds for Ping Narong. This effectively sent a message that the gem smuggling trade was now exclusively Ping's domain.

This earned Ramonne a million baht. Exactly the same million baht that had, for a brief moment, been Nit's. Ping was happy. Ramonne was happy.

Ramonne seized an opportunity and moved into Nit's Patpong apartment. He still kept the godown in Klong Toey, figuring that two safe houses might come in handy. Loh was commissioned again, and he hired a small crew to move a new coffin, sealed in an anonymous wooden crate, into the sixth-floor apartment. There was much grumbling and cursing when it was determined that the crate would not fit into the elevator. Two weeks later, Ramonne received instructions to hit the Interior vice minister.

———

Prichada had been informed that Ramonne was taking Nit's place.

Her thoughts when she delivered the first envelope assured Ramonne that she knew nothing. She was merely an errand girl. She received the envelopes and a cash payment and waited for Nit, now Ramonne, to collect it.

Though Ramonne still lusted for her, he cooled it and let her do her job.

Nit's apartment had a telephone—a device Ramonne had lived 175 years with hardly ever using—connected to an answering machine. It would receive a cryptic message—*The card game is on tonight*—when there was an envelope to be picked up.

Ramonne was actually excited to get the first one. He realized it was his first *job* in over fifty years, since he'd run the Oriental's jazz bar.

He took the envelope to the top of the Dusit Thani Hotel and climbed out onto the roof. He opened it in complete privacy.

The hit was a challenge. The minister traveled in a convoy of three armor-plated vehicles with two armed bodyguards in each. There was a schedule attached of the minister's movements for the next three days and nights.

Ramonne had thoroughly enjoyed planning and carrying out the assassination. He received his payment, 3 million baht, in a bowling alley three floors over Siam Square. He had the severed head in a bowling bag, and exchanged it for a bag full of cash.

10
____

The young girl moved among the weavers. They worked the silk through the looms and spun intricate patterns. For the little girl it was magic. The houses along Klong Saen Saep were all connected, and their open windows allowed the breezes from the canal to circulate and cool the women.

Kanchana sat on the wood floor. She was fascinated with the feet. Large, bare feet, many adorned with silver rings, working the loom pedals, producing a humming sound that she could still hear in her head today, twenty years later.

She heard the sound now as she stalked her prey. Of course, it wasn't the gentle sound of her youth but an annoying electrical generator providing power to a string of yellow bulbs and a refrigerator full of beer. She sat on the roof of a small house next to a makeshift bar set up on the *klong* that divided Thonburi down the middle.

As she waited for one of the half-dozen drunken men to get up from his plastic chair and stagger home, she allowed her mind to wander back once more to memories of her idyllic youth. Her mother ran a silk empire. She employed nearly 300 weavers. Twice a year she traveled abroad. She had three showrooms in Bangkok, one in Chiang Mai, and distributors in Paris,

New York, and Milan. Her father was a law professor, who also helped with the administrative end of the business.

Her happiest moments were visiting the weavers. These proud women greeted her beautiful mother like visiting royalty. After an hour or so, her mother would take her and her sister by the hand and they'd climb back in her private boat and fly down the canal to the river. The boat roaring along the inner waterway, the breeze blowing through her schoolgirl hair. They'd stop at the Rachinee Pier and the Pak Klong Market for vanilla ice-cream cones. Then they'd re-board the handsome craft for the journey back to their waterfront home in Thonburi.

Magical times.

That was before the decline in her mother's health. Before her father's suicide. Before her sister succumbed to the ravishing family curse.

Kanchana shuddered. And then the memory faded as she saw a lone man make his apologies to the group and stagger away.

Kanchana hissed quietly in anticipation as he headed her way. She waited until he was directly below, and then she leapt.

And missed.

Kanchana was sprawled in the weeds. She looked up to find herself face-to-face with the drunkard.

"Huh?"

The *idiot* had bent down to tie his shoelace.

In an instant she was up. But in the same instant, the man had turned and fled back to the bar.

Impulsively, Kanchana started to pursue him, but then stopped.

Six of them. I could easily slaughter them, but what would I gain? I could feed on two or three at most. The others would cause attention.

Discretion. She remembered Ramonne's advice and turned and glided silently away.

————

The next evening, Loh knocked on her boudoir door. She was just arising.

"Khun Kanchana. You have a visitor."

"*Visitor*? I want no visitor. Tell whoever it is to go away."

"Actually, I did—when he came this morning. I told him you were not feeling well and that perhaps he should return this evening."

"Why on earth did you do that? Just tell him to go away."

"He's a policeman."

"Oh."

Kanchana asked Loh to have the policeman wait while she put on 'her face.'

———

She had a polite but uncomfortable conversation with a young local constable. When it was finished and the officer had left her alone, Kanchana screamed at Loh to get the car.

"*Where is he?*" Kanchana was furious and she spit the words at Charoen.

Looking innocent, Charoen replied, "Where is who?"

"Ramonne of course."

Charoen shook his head. "I don't know. Truly I don't." He turned toward Loh, who was his usual somnambulant self.

"Surely *he* knows."

Kanchana sneered. "Oh, he knows all right. He's his hand-maiden. But he's under a spell. Sworn to secrecy. To top it off—" She motioned to Loh, who pulled open his collar, revealing a silver amulet. "He's wearing *that*. I can't touch the little bastard."

Without a change of expression, Loh closed his collar.

"Interesting. Under a spell to serve, and yet protected from those he serves. Smart little man."

"Oh yes, he's *chalaad maak*. Very clever. With personality to match."

"Why do you want Ramonne."

"I need to talk to him. This territorial thing he devised. It isn't working."

"Oh?"

"I had an…*accident*. Someone saw me and got away. The police came to my house. It was very uncomfortable."

"I see."

"No. No you don't *see*. You're blind."

Charoen stopped smiling.

"I can't be confined to Thonburi. It's too small. And now they're looking for a female. Fortunately they're not sure what she was up to, and Loh has been disposing of the bodies. But it's just a matter of time before I'm caught in a net."

Charoen smiled again. "I'm afraid that I cannot help."

Kanchana moved closer to the little man. She hissed. "You can help. You *must* help. Or else—" She started for the gnome's neck, but then stopped.

Charoen fingered the silver amulet and smiled his silly Cheshire cat grin.

Kanchana looked from Charoen to Loh. One was grinning, the other was frozen.

She howled like a banshee and then flew to Charoen's rack of potions. She flung her arm out, and dozens of beakers and vials crashed to the floor, spraying foul liquids and shards of glass. She continued her rant and rave until the entire first floor of Charoen's shophouse was destroyed.

Then she leapt to the top of the house and across the canal and was gone.

———

The top of the Rama III Bridge was 300 feet from the water's surface. On the bridge, a stream of red lights traveled east and west. On the river itself, a long convoy of sand barges passed under the bridge. They were empty, floating high in the water.

A single family lived on board each one, pulled by a determined tugboat. They were on their way upriver to Sri Sagchanalai. Each tug pulled at least eight barges, stretching a half-mile behind it. When they returned, a week from now, they would be full of sand and sit twenty feet deeper in the water.

Powerful arc lights shone upward on each side of the bridge, illuminating the graceful network of cables that held the massive structure in place. The lights also illuminated a figure at the very apex of one of the stanchions. A female.

Kanchana stared blanky into space. Tears streamed down her face, taking streaks of mascara with them. She might be a vampire, but she was still a female. She hugged her knees and emitted a dark wail, long, steady, and plaintive...and out of human range.

Her sad song carried through the night, across the river, through the canyons of the city of ten million souls.

Ramonne sat atop the Asia Bank Tower, known as the Robot Building. Its Japanese anime design had been deemed revolutionary a couple of decades back. But Ramonne thought it a disgusting monstrosity. He drained a bottle of Valpolicela. He'd gotten bored waiting for another assignment, so he'd indulged his fancy, now that he could afford it again.

He'd dined early—a pothead on Khao San Road. His bloodlust satisfied, he had gone on to the Gardens of Babylon for a couple of hours of fucking. Two girls went upstairs with him and opened their bag of tricks, like a doctor on house call, except that their bag held double-headed dildos, water solvent lubricants, handcuffs, and condoms.

On his perch, high above the city, Ramonne roared with laughter. It was good to be alive, or whatever, again.

It was almost 4:00 a.m. when he finished the wine. He was about to fling the bottle, when he heard it...

The sound carried across the night to his vampire ears. He cocked his head and stood. It coursed through him. He felt the pain, the misery, the fear…the *loneliness*.

He listened and then he emitted a low, long howl. He continued for minutes, stopping only when he had to breathe. He kept the level low enough that *she* wouldn't hear.

But that didn't stop Ramonne from responding, at least within himself. That didn't stop him from feeling.

They were together again.

There was magic in the air. The city was alive. Martin was alive.

The whole world was alive.

They caroused. They prowled. A beer garden beckoned in the warm night and Ramonne swept them through the gate.

Inside, an orchestra played. Wonderful music. The men and women were all dressed in formal attire, the men in coats and ties, some tuxedos and hats, the women in cocktail dresses and gowns. Gas lamps illuminated the garden, and beer flowed from massive wooden kegs into big steins.

Outside, vintage automobiles were lined up—Ford, Opel, Peugot, MG—all late 1920s, all magnificent.

Seeing the cars made Martin realize he'd left the twenty-first century, and that Ramonne had once more transported him to a finer, gentler time.

The orchestra played a tune he recognized. "Greensleeves."

How old was that? Timeless, he figured.

Ramonne had a flask of his own fine wine and was content to watch the couples pair off on the dance floor. Martin had a stein of fresh, bitter ale.

Shortly, Ramonne became distracted. He heard something. He cocked his head.

Now Martin heard it, too. A long keening.

Soon the sound overtook the music and the orchestra stopped playing. The musicians put down their instruments and listened. The people on the dance floor listened. Everyone stopped what they were doing—eating, drinking or talking—and listened.

Martin woke with a start.

God. How strange. He hadn't had a dream like that since... since he didn't know how long.

It was so real. Just as it was when Ramonne took him to Sanam Luang and they stood outside the gates to the Grand Palace and Ramonne described the coronation procession of King Chulalongkorn in 1868, and suddenly he was *there*. The street and its people...had shifted back to the nineteenth century.

It was marvelous. He was drunk on it. It was what bound him to the vampire. It was the power Ramonne had over him.

Martin lay back in the dark. He tried to go back to sleep, but he couldn't get the wail, that awful sound, out of his head. It went on and on. He tried covering his ears with a pillow.

And then he realized the sound was real.

He got up and opened the doors to the terrace. The sound was loud. As loud as in his dream.

He wondered how anyone in the city could sleep.

Now, from the opposite direction, came another sound, as if in response.

A low, mournful groan.

The two sounds blended together now, like two musical notes.

After a while, Martin closed the doors and went back inside.

It made no difference. He still heard them.

"Martin. It's four in the morning."

"I know what time it is, John. I'm sorry. Please do me this little favor."

"What?"

"Open your window and tell me what you hear."

"*What I hear*? I live just off Sukhumvit. You *know* what I hear. The fucking traffic."

"John. Please."

"All right."

A moment of silence and then Martin actually heard the sound of motorbikes.

"Like I said, Martin. The infernal traffic. Now can I go back to bed."

"Nothing unusual?"

"I'm hanging up, Martin."

"Thanks."

John lived less than four blocks from Martin.

Martin still heard the music of the children of the night.

He tried earplugs. He tried the digital, sound-suppressing headphones he used on airplanes.

Nothing stopped the sound.

Not until first one, and then both, stopped of their own accord.

11

The sound stopped.

Hardly anyone who wasn't Muslim heard it anymore. Three times a day. Broadcast through the town over tinny loudspeakers. People went about their daily business in ignorant bliss.

Ignorance. Our greatest weapon. Mestaphel raised himself from the kneeling position he'd just been in for his morning prayers. He looked out of the guesthouse window and watched the shopkeepers preparing for the morning's business. It was barely light yet.

The bus from the Malaysian border town of Pedang Besar had been the vessel chosen for him and his glorious journey. He had gotten off the bus in Hat Yai, where he had hired a taxi to take him here, to the town of Satun to the west. He had thought about spending the night with the infidels in their sin parlors, as many Malays did in their regular visits to Hat Yai, but there would be time enough for that when he reached Bangkok.

Mestaphel did his toilet and walked downstairs. His little hotel was at the end of Samantha Prasit Road. The red-eyed clerk with the breath of a pig told him it was about a ten-minute walk to the Bambang Mosque in the center of town.

He walked the dusty street and soon he was surrounded by

Muslim food shops. He chose a little café and settled in for his morning repast.

Refreshed and fed, he glanced at his watch. It was time. He paid the small bill and crossed the street to the gold-domed mosque. Two turbaned men stood on either side of the door. They bowed to him and he raised a hand in greeting. Though nothing was visible, it was obvious to Mestaphel that they were armed. Inside, the faithful were gathered on the cool, blue tile floor awaiting the weekly news. The doors were locked. Mestaphel smiled.

God is great.

———

Four hours later, in the blistering heat of the noonday sun, Mestaphel was once again heading north. He felt satisfied and content. He had witnessed first hand the delivery of the message they received in their safe house in Malacca. This was a weekly occurrence in mosques throughout southern Thailand. Chosen ones traveled north and delivered weekly oratories against their enemies in the great war, and uplifting news from the front lines where the leaders of Al Qaeda and Jamah Islamiyah plotted and carried out their war in secrecy. These reports would be circulated throughout the week to communities all over the South.

This minor duty completed, Mestaphel could carry on his true mission uninterrupted. A mission that would bring glory to his name, and his family, forever. He would allow himself a few hours sleep and put his seat back. This movement was met with protest from the huge infidel behind him, and his equally appalling water buffalo of a mate.

Mestaphel ignored them.

———

By dark they were three kilometers south of the city of Surat Thani. Mestaphel was awake and doing silent prayers when he felt the bus start to slow down. He stiffened in his seat as he saw a flashing red light atop a large, free-standing sign to the left of the highway. The words were indecipherable but Mestaphel knew what it meant.

Road block. A police checkpoint.

Ever since the great bombings in Bali and Saudi Arabia, all of Southeast Asia, and Thailand in particular, had been on warning lists issued by the Western nations. The Thai prime minister had insisted his country was safe and that extraordinary measures were being taken to safeguard the lives of all law-abiding citizens, foreign workers, and tourists. Especially tourists, whom, it was assumed, would constitute any likely target. Airport security was heightened, local police combined with government forces to patrol entertainment places, and roadblocks were set up on all major highways.

Mestaphel's great journey had deliberately been postponed until after the Christmas and New Year high season to allow for an expected lessening of these measures. Now that he was faced with his first police encounter, Mestaphel wasn't sure what to feel. He noticed the other passengers shifting in their seats, rummaging through handbags, retrieving passports and other documents for the expected questions to come.

Mestaphel looked at his Malay passport. Although it was in actuality less than two months old, it was well worn, reflecting the life and times of the merchant that the piece of misinformation had turned him into.

If they only knew.

And just in case they did know, in the far-removed possibility that his real identity had been discovered, and that a piece of paper was now being circulated with his picture on it and, by chance, a copy of that document had ended up here in this Godforsaken highway outpost, then there was the Beretta in his pocket. He would take great pleasure in shooting the fat German couple behind him before taking his own life.

God is great.

But as the bus approached the police stand, it was clear that a stop was not necessary. The young uniformed officer sat behind a folding table, a thirty-inch television set tuned to a soccer match. He was slumped in his chair, sound asleep.

The driver shifted gears and proceeded up the highway. Mestaphel relaxed, letting his seat recline again into the German's kneecap.

———

"Mai pen rai?"

"Mai pen rai." No problems. Mestaphel answered back in one of the few Thai phrases he knew.

He was glad to be off the God-damned bus, even though—as promised to one as great as he—it had been air-conditioned. Persons of his status had made the same journey before in the comfort of a chauffer-driven Mercedes. But of course, since the glorious victory of September 11, all the great patriots' movements were much more clandestine, passing unnoticed under the infidels' radar.

He was met in Bangkok by Khun Yai, a Thai Muslim who was to be "trusted completely."

"His neck, my knife." Mestaphel silently chanted an old saying.

At this point Mestaphel didn't care if he was met by Satan himself—not if he'd take him to a clean room with a real bed and no fat Germans behind it. He had gotten very close—*very fucking close*—to slitting the German pig's throat while he snored; a sound akin to the belching of a thousand Turks.

He followed as Khun Yai loaded his bags onto a cart and directed a sleepy porter through the bus terminal to a sorry, twenty-year-old Volvo.

"Okay?"

It was not okay. But it would do.

Mestaphel reminded himself he was undercover. Deep undercover. He sighed and climbed into the run-down car.

Allah, the sacrifices we make.

———

An hour later, Mestaphel lay on the solid mattress of one of the twin beds in his utilitarian room.

Why don't they just put four pockets in the corners and we could shoot billiards?

He wondered about the slate-like composition of the bed. Finally he pulled off the single fitted sheet and discovered that the bed was in fact constructed of shredded coconut husks, pressed into a solid bale.

He stared up at the bare fluorescent tube. A little refrigerator made an annoying noise in the corner, trying to keep a miserable selection of beer and sodas lukewarm. The bathroom had a toilet that constantly, incessantly 'ran' after he had used it once. And the TV, circa 1954, got three channels of Thai-language programs—childish game shows and military propaganda—and these were covered in 'snow.'

Oh, the infidels will pay for this.

———

A week went by. He heard nothing.

He expected this. They were making sure that he was clean. He didn't mind. He had never been to Bangkok before. What a city. He hired a car and discovered that it had no end. No matter which direction he went, the city went on forever. The driver was mystified by his lack of a destination. "Just drive." He said it like Jack Nicholson. He liked Jack Nicholson movies. He liked Jack.

Perhaps Jack could be spared?

He'd ask. Couldn't hurt.

At night he'd hang around the hotel. The Lux was Vietnam-War-era, Indian run, and had an all-night coffee shop whose main attribute seemed to be the low-rent hookers who congregated there after 2:00 a.m.

Mestaphel was reminded of Manila, where he had lived for a year in his guise as a metals trader, while organizing the aborted bomb attack against the demon pope. If all had gone as planned, he would have strapped the explosives onto the chosen one, who would have incinerated the great Pious Satan, and soon been received at the holy gates by 72 blessed virgins.

A wonderful 'entertainment center' was a short walk away from his Manila hotel, and he soon had a little whore from the Firehouse disco as his full-time sex slave. He fucked at night and worked all day for the great cause. Alas, a chemical error set their safe house on fire in their absence one day, and—unbelievably—they were busted by the Philippine police. Mestaphel was with his girlfriend at the time, in a 'love hotel,' and managed to flee the country unnoticed.

The hookers in the Lux coffee shop were a little rough for Mestaphel's taste. He had a wife who had born him six children, and he greatly appreciated younger women with no scars on their bellies from Caesareans, no stretch marks from multiple births.

He would wander on down Sukhumvit Road at night and encounter various amateurs—schoolgirls looking to supplement their allowance; secretaries; sales clerks—all those who had suffered the Big Bust's trickle-down effect. He'd choose a ripe one and take her back to his horrid little room.

Funny, they never once complained about the décor.

———

Exactly one week after arriving in Bangkok, a city he now realized was as complicated as the Rubik's Cube he'd wasted hundreds of youthful hours upon, he received his first official order.

Khun Yai approached as he was having breakfast in the coffee shop.

"Yes?"

"All is ready."

Mestaphel dropped his croissant and dismissed last night's whore.

———

Ten blocks and an hour later, Khun Yai pulled into a narrow *soi* off Sukhumvit 3, opposite Bumrungrad Hospital, and stopped outside the gated entry to a private home. A uniformed guard saluted and opened the gate. Khun Yai parked the car.

"I'll stay with the car."

That suited Mestaphel fine. An hour in the atmosphere of Khun Yai—cheap cologne, sweat, and some kind of pickle— was enough. He needed a break.

He walked up the steps to the door and left his shoes next to the half-dozen others at the entrance. The doors were opened by a turbaned man who bowed and pointed to a set of closed doors across a spacious foyer. Mestaphel followed the man, who opened both doors at once.

"Ahhh. Mestaphel. Welcome." He was greeted in Pashto, the language of Afghanistan. He was hugged and kissed on both cheeks. "I am Mon. It is a pleasure to finally make your acquaintance. I trust your journey was comfortable?"

"Yes. It was fine."

"Please be seated. Have some tea."

There were three other men seated around the low, circular brass table. Mon joined them. No other introductions were made. Mestaphel was not surprised.

Anonymity is our greatest strength. Who and what you don't know can't be used against you.

He knew this was why Khun Yai stayed with the car. Staying in the dark kept him alive.

In the course of the next three hours, a plot was laid that, once executed, would change the face of Bangkok, the fate of Thailand, and shape the destiny of Southeast Asia for decades to come.

12

"He frequents these dens of iniquity?"

Lieutenant-Colonel Samarat seemed amused.

"He does." Martin was not.

He was in the back seat of a cop car—again. Back where it all began that fateful night that seemed so long ago.

Areeya was seated next to him. He wasn't sure why, but it just seemed that having someone else who had actually seen the vampire and knew what he was capable of would help him get his point across.

They were on Soi 13, outside the Gardens of Babylon.

"Stay here, please. Sergeant, come with me."

Samarat got out of the car and went inside the club with the driver, Sergeant Manat.

"What are we doing?" Areeya asked.

"Looking. For traces. For evidence that he's back."

"I thought you had evidence. He showed you pictures."

"There's a vampire in Bangkok, all right. I want to be sure it's him."

"And if it isn't?"

"If it isn't him, then it's none of my business."

Areeya looked out the window. The little *soi* was wall-to-wall bars. Their neon signs seemed to beckon to her.

"Man, do I want a drink."

'This is good for you. Face your demons from the safety of a police car."

"I'm not handcuffed, Martin."

"That could be arranged."

"Hmmmm." She studied him. Was he flirting with her? She couldn't be sure. It'd been *so long.* He was kind of cute in a dorky sort of way.

"Why's your hair so short?"

"I was in a monastery, remember?"

"Oh yeah. Have you got a cigarette?"

"Don't smoke."

"Neither do I. Look, let's say he is back…then what?"

"Then—"

Samarat climbed back in the car. "Well?"

"Khun Fritz wasn't too happy to have 'ze police' in his establishment. But he co-operated."

"And?"

"Your man's been there. Twice this week."

Martin sank back in the seat.

That's it. It starts again.

"I told him to call me if and when he returns."

"What do we do now?" Areeya crossed her arms and looked at Martin.

"I'm not sure. What we did before must not have worked. Or it was only temporary. I don't know."

"Who does?" Samarat leaned back and put the question directly to Martin.

It was Areeya who answered. "There *is* someone."

———

"*Manananggal* in the Philippines, *phii dib* here in Thailand. The people believe in these spirits, and their legends are widespread. There is truth and untruth as in all legends. They do exist, the wandering spirits; usually the spirits of those who suffer violent, untimely deaths. They are trapped between the present and the neverworld. They wander the land until they are reunited with their souls and they can return to the wheel in peace. These spirits can be easily pacified or dispersed. There are many potions and spells to deal with them." Charoen swept his hand toward his collection of bottles and beakers, greatly reduced by Kanchana's fit of pique, but back in order.

"These spirits have relatively short life spans and limited physical powers." He smiled.

The smile sent a chill through Martin. He, Areeya, and Samarat were in Charoen's lower parlor. Sergeant Manat was with the car.

"However, the one you seek is all-powerful. He has the physical strength of ten men, he is impervious to pain, he can withstand assault by any of your weapons."

"Bullshit," Samarat commented.

"It's true. You—" Charoen turned to Martin. "You know this to be true, do you not."

"Yes. I've seen bullets pass through him. However, I...I have seen what a shotgun at close range can do."

"On hallowed ground was it not?" Charoen reached into a drawer in the table at which they sat.

"Yes. Wat Arun."

"He *is* vulnerable on hallowed ground."

"Then how is it possible that he is back? I saw him burned into ash."

"Khun Martin. I can tell that you have recently been on a long spiritual journey. I know you believe now in reincarnation."

"Yes."

"Then why would not this one also be reincarnated?"

"I can't imagine it was that simple."

"No, Khun Martin, I don't imagine it was *simple* either. Or without pain."

Martin felt another chill. *What does this fortune-teller really know?*

"You seek wisdom." Charoen produced a book. Not the same as the books that Ramonne took, but similar in age and appearance. Also in Braille.

"Wisdom comes with a price."

Martin sighed and got out his wallet.

Charoen smiled. "I doubt you have enough in your wallet for what I'm about to teach you. Do you perhaps have your checkbook?"

For the sum of 100,000 baht they were treated to two hours of lectures on sun exposure, beheading, beheading with garlic stuffed into the head, cutting out and burning of the heart, cremation and scattering the ashes. Perhaps, Martin thought, that was the simple flaw in what he had done before; he didn't *scatter* the ashes. And Charoen affirmed that the vampire could be regenerated from a mere sliver—though exactly *how*, he professed not to know. There was also cutting the body open and washing it with boiling wine. Stakes through the heart were not reliable—and any such attempt would probably waken the sleeping vampire; never a good idea.

When he was done, the charlatan had Martin's head spinning. Martin would have to sort through this new wealth of vampire knowledge and compare it with what he had been told by Jonathan Peyton.

"Before you leave, I have one more item that might be of use to you."

Charoen reached into the drawer again and withdrew a silver talisman on a leather string.

"This will provide protection from the vampire." Martin scoffed. "You expect us to believe that?"

Charoen opened his collar and pulled out his own amulet.

"Yes. I do."

Martin picked it up.

"How much?"

———

When they were gone, Charoen went about the business of closing up the shophouse.

"Jar." *Where is that worthless maggot?*

He thought the evening had gone well. He'd gotten another 40,000 baht for the amulet. How wise of Loh to not do the vampire's original bidding and drop the amulets in the river. And he only had to pay Loh 1,000 baht to get it back. That was a 39,000-baht tidy profit. *Not bad.*

He had no idea what they would do with the information. Maybe they'd catch the vampire. Maybe they'd destroy him. Maybe. It didn't matter anymore. Ramonne was becoming a nuisance. And after all, it wasn't like Ramonne was the only vampire in Bangkok now. No. Charoen had his own little vampire—Kanchana. A *young* vampire. Much easier to control. And he *would* control her. Oh yes.

"Jar. What are you doing?" He felt the servant's presence and put out a hand to touch him. "You're very cold."

'And soon you will be even colder.'

He's here? Why did I not know?

'Because I didn't want you to know, you traitorous little worm.'

The voice was in his head. He wanted it out. Out of his head. Out of his house.

"Where are you?"

"Can't you see me?"

"No. I feel you, but I don't know where you are…Jar! Where is he?"

"I'm afraid your faithful servant has found another master."

Jar stood in the room, vacant-eyed. Charoen reached out to him again. He felt the man's face.

"Jar. What is wrong with you? Speak to me." He felt for the man's hand. He recoiled as he touched it.

"What's *that*? A knife?"

"Afraid so, little man," Ramonne replied.

Charoen backed up. He fingered the talisman around his neck. "I don't fear you."

"Oh. But you should."

"Jar."

The servant held the knife stiffly in front of him as he approached the shaman, grabbing his master by the neck.

"Jar. What are you doing?"

Charoen was backed into a corner. Jar extended the knife. Charoen grabbed for it and the blade sliced his hand. Blood flowed down his arm as he tried to stop the attack. With his other hand Jar grabbed the strap of the talisman. Charoen could not stop the thrust of the blade. It sliced through the strap and the amulet fell to the floor.

Immediately, Jar stopped and the blade returned to his side.

"Pick it up, Jar."

Charoen's bloody fingers searched frantically for the talisman, but Jar already had it.

"Good. Now walk to the window."

Jar did as told.

"Throw it in the canal."

Again, Jar did as instructed.

"Ahhh. That's better."

"Please. I mean you no harm. I…I created you."

"You mean me no harm? You just sold me to the coppers." Ramonne sneered. "And don't ever think you had anything to do with 'creating' me. I was born a man, in God's image. As all men are. If anything, you merely rejuvenated me."

Ramonne was in Charoen's face. He sniffed. He smiled. He smelled fear.

"And as I've said before, *who asked you to*?"

Ramonne opened the drawer in the table. "Not me, that's for sure."

He withdrew the book. "Holding out on me, Charoen?"

"No. Of course not. This book says the same as the ones I gave you."

Ramonne ran his hands over a few pages. "Not quite. There's more here. Much more." He closed the book and set it on the table.

"You know, Charoen. I really didn't come here to kill you."

"Thank you."

"But now I *am* going to kill you. Make no mistake about that."

There was nothing but a moaning sound from the shaman.

"I came here to ask you a question about Kanchana. I've been reading the books you gave me, and I have a theory. It seems that the simple act of making her a vampire has most likely destroyed all traces of cancerous cells in her."

Charoen was sweating profusely. "No doubt."

"And, if I'm not mistaken, a very young vampire is unstable. True?"

"How…how so?"

"They are not completely transformed in the first three months; they're unstable. They have human emotions, human needs. They still hunger for food. Women can suffer menstruation."

"I suppose that I read that, yes."

"Then, in theory, she could be changed back. Restored to her mortal self and be cured. Free of her disease."

"In theory, yes."

"But how?"

"I have no idea."

Ramonne was back in Charoen's face.

"Oh you have an idea. *I feel it.* Tell me, would you prefer a quick painless death, or would you like to be impaled? The way one of my 'ancestors' would do?"

For a horrible moment, Charoen saw his own terrible demise, skewered like a pig, the stake going in his anus and coming out through his throat.

He screamed and the image disappeared.

"All right. There might be a way."

"Ahh. Now you're being sensible."

———

Charoen was dead. Ramonne placed him in a trance and drank of his blood. Quickly. Painlessly.

Ramonne walked out the front door with the leather satchel he had brought with him. In it was the book and a selection of other items that Charoen had thoughtfully provided for his task.

Ramonne instructed the silent servant Jar to douse the shophouse with gasoline, set it ablaze, and then slit his own throat. Jar *waied* and assured him that all would be done.

Ramonne watched and then walked down the alley as the flames rose behind him.

13

From his apartment window, Ramonne watched the street vendors wrap up Patpong for the night. He thought about going out for a snack, but he was too tired. Exhausted. Tonight had been more than he had bargained for.

He had been upstairs at the shaman's when the police car pulled up. He had just finished hypnotizing the hapless manservant Jar, and he stole to window.

Who should exit the car with the police? Martin.

Martin!

And the girl, Yaya.

Ramonne was so excited he had almost gone downstairs and slashed the policeman's throat and given Martin a bear hug. Instead he had stayed in the shadows upstairs and watched while Charoen taught a class in Vampire Destruction 101. Fascinating. So many things he still didn't know. So many things Charoen had forgotten to teach him.

All the while, he kept staring at Martin. How good it was to see him. He looked well. Had Lost weight. Nice tan. He was too far away to actually read Martin's thoughts, but just seeing him had made him feel good. He tried to project the thought that he bade him no ill will for what had transpired. After all, he had planned his own demise. Martin was merely a pawn.

But Ramonne cancelled that idea as he realized that they—all of them—were conspiring to eradicate him. Again.

Ungrateful bastards, he had thought at the time.

He re-thought that and wasn't sure why they *should* be grateful.

Just *bastards*, then.

The idea of a roomful of people conspiring to bring about his demise was depressing, and he was glad when Martin and company left, so that he could have the pleasure of killing one of them.

Ramonne was returned to the present by a sound.

Her cry.

Her lonely, lonely cry.

He sighed. Tonight he would not respond. He was just too tired.

Soon. Soon I will set you free.

He climbed into the coffin.

Life had suddenly become so complicated.

He closed the lid. In the darkened room the little red message light on the answering machine blinked on and off.

On and off.

———

Martin lay awake, staring at the ceiling.

On the ride back from the shaman's, they'd discussed strategy. Samarat was humoring them at best, he decided. But at least he was entertaining the idea that there might be a vampire on the loose in his town.

Martin argued that, in spite of the romance of ideas like stuffing his head full of garlic—you had to have the head first, he pointed out—and removing his heart, there still seemed one or two practical ways of dealing with Ramonne. One was to find where he spent his days, go there in the daylight hours, behead him while he slept, and drag the corpse and head—with or without it being stuffed with garlic—to hallowed ground and let the sun destroy the body. This time, make sure that all ashes were scattered to the wind. That nothing remained.

The other plan, only a slight variation, would be to stalk him as before with shotguns, blow his head off, and drag the body parts to hallowed ground.

Samarat said that, since they had no idea where he was spending his days, but at least had some idea where he spent his nights, Plan B seemed appropriate.

But Martin would not be getting a shotgun. Only Samarat and his officers would bear arms. No innocent citizens would go down on his watch.

Martin reluctantly agreed, and they decided to start in earnest tomorrow night.

Outside Areeya's apartment, Martin had put the talisman around her neck.

"Don't take it off. Not at night."

"I won't."

She watched as he turned to go and then she reached out and pulled him to her. She kissed him. Not too hard, not too long. But long enough to get his attention.

As he walked back to the car, Martin remembered what Charoen said when Martin asked if he had another talisman: "No. But Martin, your best protection is to remain holy."

Remain holy.

He'd been celibate for over a year, but right then he was so aroused, he had trouble even sitting down. How would he remain holy?

He tried to go to sleep.

And then he heard the cry once more.

Great. No sleep again.

He sat bolt upright.

Trace the cry. Follow it and you'll find Ramonne.

Quickly he got dressed.

————

"Right. Turn right."

"But that's the bridge to Chom Thong, sir," the driver warned.

"I know. Just please turn right."

Martin had followed the sound for a half-hour. Twice around Lumpini Park until he realized he had to go south on Sathorn Road. The driver was certain his passenger was completely *baa*. The taxi driver heard no unusual sound.

As they approached the bridge, the sound grew much louder.

Martin looked around. His head was out the window, like a dog going for a ride.

Where?

Then he saw it.

"Stop!"

"I can't stop on the bridge, sir."

"It's four in the morning. Just pull over."

Reluctantly the driver did as Martin asked.

"I can't stay here, sir."

Martin handed the man a few 100-baht notes and got out.

The green and yellow taxi pulled away immediately.

Martin stood and looked up. The figure was midway up the stanchion of the elegant suspension bridge, 200 feet away. It looked alone and forlorn. It continued its mournful wail.

"Shit." Martin started up a steep ladder, climbing hand over hand to a perpendicular steel beam. It was about six feet wide. He was a quarter of the way and frozen with fright. He looped his arm through the ladder and sat on the beam, straddling it.

The figure noticed him and immediately began a descent. It leaped and clung to a cable. It used that to drop down onto the beam that Martin clung to. It had made a 100-foot descent in a matter of seconds. It approached him slowly, back-lit by the arc light shining up the bridge. Martin could not make out the face. But the silhouette told him it wasn't Ramonne.

"Who are you?" The figure stopped.

"Who are *you*?" Martin replied, clinging on.

The figure moved and the light caught the face for a moment.

Martin almost let go his grasp in shock.

It's a woman.

The face was young but torn with despair. Dried tears mixed with mascara ran down each side of the gaunt face. Her jet-black hair was windblown and framed the small face like coils of a snake. She seemed frightened, nervous, and hung back in the shadows.

She's a vampire.

Martin's rational mind told him to climb back down, jump in the water, get away.

"What are you doing up here?" Her voice was dry and raspy.

"I followed the sound. Your cry."

"You *heard* me? Impossible."

"I heard you last night, also. It woke me."

"Only *he* can hear me. Unless—" She approached Martin. She studied him, sniffed, and retreated.

"You're mortal."

"Yes."

"Do you know who I am?"

"No. But I know *what* you are."

"How?"

"I knew…I *know* him. I heard his answer to your cry last night."

"He *answered* me? I did not hear him. How could you?"

"I don't know. I didn't know until now that there were two of you. I came here looking for him."

She had moved closer now. Somehow Martin did not feel

threatened by her. Still, she *was* a vampire, and he was prepared to drop into the river if that became necessary.

Hell. The fall will kill you.

"You *knew* him? Before?"

"Yes. Before."

"And he didn't…kill you?" She cocked her head like a bird.

"No. He offered to—"

"Make you one of us?"

"Yes."

"And?"

"We betrayed each other. I am the one who destroyed him."

Martin was certain he would have to leap. He started to shift his weight, but she remained immobile. Calm, even.

"So it was you. He told me about you."

"He did?"

"Yes. He did not grant you the gift, but I think he gave you something. I think you are a *medium*. This is why you can *hear* us."

Martin pondered this. If it were true, then finding Ramonne would be possible.

"You are lucky," she said. "Very lucky. You don't know the hell I'm going through."

"He made you?"

"Of course. He was brought back for that purpose."

"How? Why?"

"It's a long story." She sat next to him and told her tale.

———

When she finished, Martin was in shock. "Good Lord. You wander Thonburi, and Ramonne is in Bangkok?"

"Yes. That's how he wants it. But I have stopped feeding. It…it disgusts me."

She turned her head away.

Martin heard her quiet sobs. He had no idea what to do. No idea what to say. So he did nothing. Said nothing.

Finally she turned back to him. "I was a coward. I couldn't face death. I wanted to cheat death. I wanted to cheat the painful death I knew I was due to suffer. I had no idea that it would mean an eternity of suffering. Each morning, I wonder if this is the day I'll have the strength to stay here and face the sun. Let it destroy me."

Martin reached out. He took her hand. Instantly Kanchana recoiled, but then she relented and reached back. He took the hand. He felt it was remarkably small to hold so many troubles.

"I'll stay with you, if that'll help."

She looked into his eyes. "I want…I want to see him again."

They sat in silence as the sky started the first shift from black to blue. Then she pulled away her hand and stood.

"Find him for me, *mon cherie.*"

She leapt to the footpath below. He watched her climb over the side and use a rope to descend to a covered longtail boat waiting there for her. It roared away, shooting a giant tail plume of water in its wake.

Martin slept through the day. He had turned off his phone, and when he awoke there were three messages.

He showered and made a cup of tea before he listened to them.

"Khun Larue. It's Colonel Samarat. Call me."

"Martin. It's Yaya. Funny, I haven't used that name for months. I was afraid to. But I think maybe I can be Yaya again… with you. My protector." There was a slight laugh and a short pause. "It's noon. Do you want to have lunch? Call me."

He looked at his watch. Five o'clock.

"Damn." He dialed her number. It rang three times and then the answering machine picked up.

"Areeya. It's Martin. Listen, you're not going to believe—"

She answered.

"What could you tell me that I wouldn't believe? I'm a 'believer,' remember?"

"Okay. Sorry about lunch. But I had the most amazing experience after I left you." He told her about meeting— *What's her name? She never told me*—the female vampire.

"I think I can find Ramonne. I think I can *sense* him. I don't know why, but I'm starting to think anything is possible. But, Areeya, this woman…she was really sad."

There was a long pause. Finally, "I don't know how to react to that. She's a vampire, Martin. What's your plan?"

"I don't know. I haven't gotten that far."

"Hmmm. I assume this means we're going out tonight."

"Areeya—"

"Yaya."

"Sorry, Yaya…you don't have to—"

"Don't. You leave me alone and I'm getting a case of champagne and a pound of Columbian coke."

Martin smiled. She probably would.

"All right. As soon as I know what I'm doing I'll come and get you."

"I'll be here…Martin?"

"Yeah?"

"Nothing."

He pressed the button and the last message played. The digital read-out told him it had come in just over an hour ago.

"Martin. It's me again. Samarat. Where are you? We've got to talk. It seems…it seems there's more than one."

Shit.

"Meet me at the station by seven o'clock. If you're not here, I'll send someone to get you."

14

———

Martin ignored the cop. Right now he wanted to find Ramonne. Not necessarily destroy him. At least not without talking to him.

Areeya drove.

"Do you think it was wise to ignore Samarat?"

"I don't know about 'wise.'" Martin realized that he was beginning to be his old confused self again. "I don't know about a lot of things. Like your name, for instance. Which is it? Yaya or Areeya?"

"Which do you prefer?"

"Areeya."

"Then it's Areeya." A long moment passed while she made quick sidelong glances at him, trying to read his eyes. Then, "Where are we going?"

"He had a place. It was special to him. Maybe it still is."

———

Areeya parked the car on the side *soi* off Silom and they walked around the corner to the entrance to an old cemetery.

They stood outside. The gate was open.

"Well? Is he here?"

"How the hell would I know?"

"Martin. You said you could *sense* him."

"I said I *thought* I could sense him. Now I'm not so sure. Let's go inside."

"Oh, sure. I'm not doing drugs or drinking. Now it's cemeteries at midnight. I've progressed."

Inside, the cemetery was exactly as Martin remembered it. Crosses and other religious symbols set askew atop gravestones and crypts. Most of the graves were unkempt. In the center was a large mausoleum with the name "Hernando" carved over the entry.

The gate to the mausoleum was open.

"He's here."

"You feel him?"

Areeya took his hand and squeezed it. "I see him."

Ramonne stepped out of the shadows of the mausoleum.

"Hello boy."

Martin immediately sensed the power of the vampire, both mental and physical, as he approached.

'I see you brought a date. How charming.'

"Don't thought project. Just talk. Okay? This is Areeya. Remember her?"

"Oh yes. That miserable little man's charming daughter. Delighted to see you again, my dear."

Areeya just nodded. She was frozen with fear.

"Martin, just one more thought reading and then I'll stop. I know how much it annoys you, but your friend here is quite surprised that you found me so easily."

Areeya's jaw dropped. "How did you know that?"

"I read your mind."

"I'm pretty amazed I found you this quickly, also. I just had a hunch you might be here."

"*A hunch?* You think you found me because you had a hunch? Martin, I led you here. I arranged to be found."

"Why?"

"Why did you come looking for me? We need to talk."

Areeya finally gained control over her legs and started to back slowly away. "You know, I can see you two have a lot of catching up to do. I'll…I'll just wait in the car."

"Good idea." Ramonne smiled.

"No. Stay. He won't hurt you…us. Will you?" Ramonne seemed to ponder this for a moment.

"*Will you?*"

"No. I was just playing with you. But Martin, I do think it's better if she does wait in the car."

Areeya nodded. "So do I. You guys probably want to talk about girls and stuff."

She backed to the gate and was gone.

"Nice girl. I always liked her."

"You should have apologized for killing her father."

"Never. I wish I could kill him again."

"Typical."

"No 'Hey Ramonne, how the hell are you? Good to have you back. How *did* you get back, by the way?' Last time you saw me, I was turned to fucking ash. *Ash!*"

"I had to do that."

"Yes. You did. I made you do it."

"I know. And I know about your regeneration."

"What do you know?"

"Everything. I saw *her*."

"Kanchana?"

"If that's her name, yes."

"Where was she?"

"On top of the Rama III Bridge. That's where she spends her nights now. Calling to you."

"I hear her."

"So do I."

"You do?"

"Yes."

"Martin, just let me read your thoughts for a minute or two. It will cut through about an hour of question and answer."

"No. Talking is good. You and I came to an agreement about that a long time ago."

"Before I was destroyed."

"Doesn't matter. You're still the same."

"Except for the touch of gray. Rather distinguished, don't you think?"

"You look like Jay Leno."

"Who?"

"Never mind. She's very sad. Kanchana."

"Yes, she is. I realize now that this is what would have happened to you. I think you were ready. *I* pulled the plug. But you would have been like her. You would have regretted the decision."

"I didn't know you could."

"I didn't either. I had no teacher. I knew very little about the art of being a vampire. But now I'm learning."

"I suppose that's a good thing?"

"Yes. You know, I think I can restore her."

"Restore her?"

"Yes. To her mortal self. Without the disease."

"What makes you think you can do that?"

"What I've read, of course. In books I got from the shaman."

"Charoen."

"Yes…I saw you there. With her and the cop."

"I thought I felt you there."

Ramonne pondered this.

"Martin, why did you come here tonight?"

"I needed to find you. Needed to talk to you."

"And?"

"And…we got in the car. We started driving and I suddenly thought of the cemetery."

"I *willed* you to come here. You heard her cries. What about my cries?"

"Heard those, too."

"You're 'tuned' to us, Martin. Again, I don't know how this happens or why, but you and I have such a history, such a bond, that you are aware of our comings and goings, when other mortals are not."

"I couldn't shut out the cries, yet no one else could hear them."

"She'll start again soon." Ramonne looked at the night sky. He appeared wistful.

"She's not feeding."

"You're concerned, Martin?"

"No. As a human being, I'm glad she's not *feeding*. But if you plan to restore her, it had better be soon. She's threatening to walk into the sun."

"I'll go to her soon."

There was a long silence. Both were lost in their own thoughts.

"What did you do with my things?"

"I auctioned it all. For charity. Generous donations went to orphanages here, Vietnam, and Cambodia."

"Hmmm. Will it make a difference?"

"A little. Yes."

Ramonne mulled this for a moment.

"All of it?"

"No. I kept some of it."

"The Van Gogh?"

"Gone."

"The Degas?"

"Gone."

"What *did* you keep?"

"The daguerreotypes. Angkor and the girl."

Giselle. He kept the photo of Giselle. "Can I have it? Just the girl. Keep the rest."

"Of course."

Another pause.

"You know I've got to bring you down again, don't you?"

"I know you told the cops about me." Ramonne's yellow eyes glowed.

Martin remembered to fear him. "When I heard you were back, I couldn't believe it. After all the horror before—"

"There were good times too, Martin. *Very* good times."

"There were. Mostly perverted, twisted...but good, yes, I'll admit it."

"I taught you things, boy. *Showed* you things. Things *no* mortal has seen."

"Yes. Yes you did. I can't deny that. But you killed people. You still kill people...unmercifully."

"Not unmercifully. If you know anything about me, you know I am merciful."

"All right. You have your own twisted set of moral values. But Lord, you regularly suck the life out of innocent victims."

"I've changed."

"Excuse me?"

"I've got a job. I no longer prey on 'innocent' victims."

"You have a *job*? What does that mean?"

"I'm a hit man. The people I kill now, they deserve to die."

"Oh God help me. You actually believe this?"

"Martin, I'm working tonight. Come with me. You'll see. This scumbag does not deserve to breathe the same air as you...and I."

"I can't believe what I'm hearing. You're inviting me to come along on a hit?"

"Yes. It'll be fun. Like old times."

"Your butchering of people is not exactly the fondest memory I have of our relationship."

"Martin."

"No. Listen. I'm leaving. This is all too much. Your being *alive*, or whatever. I have to think about all of this. But you must know, I'm in league against you. I know that you must be destroyed."

'You tried once."

"You wanted it then."

"I had no purpose."

"Oh? And as a hit man you've found religion?"

"Kind of like you. Instant karma."

"What do you mean?"

"Have you ever thought that maybe monks are the real vampires? They wander the countryside *sucking* their daily sustenance from the poor, the privileged, whoever will give them what they need to sustain their existence."

"How did you know?"

"Martin. You're an open book to me."

Martin walked to the gate. "If you know so much about me, you must know that I care for that girl out there. Don't hurt her."

"She's protected, Martin. She has one of those fucking amulets. Why didn't you keep it for yourself?"

"I didn't think I needed it."

"Don't be so sure, boy."

15

Sex.

Martin thought he'd forgotten all about it. Replaced it with thoughts of *samsara* and *anicca*. Rebirth and impermanence. Replaced masturbation with meditation. Sometime in the past year, he wasn't sure exactly when, his libido diminished. Withered and vanished. Somewhere, as his bare feet grew calloused from miles and miles of wandering, it just left. He didn't even miss it. It was a relief, actually. Instead of the typical male thought pattern—forty out of every sixty seconds, two thirds of his waking life, devoted to thoughts of lust, and that's just the waking hours; most of Martin's dreams were of the wet variety—Martin had become truly clear-headed. Able to fully concentrate for the first time in his life. It was wonderful. He analyzed his role in the universe, unimpeded by impure desires. He became one with nature. He not only felt and tasted the rain. He *was* the rain. He *was* the earth. The trees. The flowers. The shit. The sewage. All of it. He knew its true essence and reveled in the newfound knowledge and freedom. Without sex on the brain, he was able to confront his other inner demons. Face them, accept *or* reject them. Clear and clean. In the moment.

It was this level of transcendence that had allowed him to

feel free to leave the temple at Nong Pah Pong and return to his life in Bangkok. Return to the *scene of the crime*. A good and free spirit. Unburdened by lust. Ready to pursue a righteous and virtuous existence.

He had examined the Buddhist wisdom of the vow of poverty, and had decided that, in his case, since his fortune was so vast, prudence was to be observed. He would distribute the wealth, but only after careful examination of the charities and organizations that would be so very eager to acquire it. And poverty? Well, he had had internal discussions about this and concluded that the Lord Buddha had not meant it literally, and he had decided on a life that was comfortable but not ostentatious. This would suffice and, in the long run, allow him to manage the various foundations and fellowships he would establish—thus serving the greater good.

A *holy man*? A good man. Pure. No unclean thoughts. That was the plan. It had worked fine in the monastery. The nuns were removed from any and all physical contact with the monks. He had all but forgotten about sex.

Until Yaya—or was it Areeya?—had unbuttoned his shirt and ran her tongue over his chest...

They had ridden in silence from the graveyard. He had very little to say. She knew better than to press him. And she didn't want to know *too* much.

She drove to her house. It wasn't discussed. She just did it.

Once inside, she put on a kettle and made tea. Green tea. When the pot boiled she poured it into two porcelain cups and took a small whisk and stirred it to a slight froth. She cupped his with both hands and put it under Martin's nose. He was lost in thought but the earthy, pungent aroma revived him. He sat up and took the cup.

"Thanks."

She smiled and picked up her cup. "*Domo arigato.*"

Martin sipped the tea. "You spent time in Japan?"

"I went to school there for two years. After a very *bad* year here. Don't ask, okay."

"Okay." He looked at her. She didn't avoid his gaze. "It's just that you're so…so—"

"Young?"

"Yes."

She moved to the couch and sat next to him. "Youth, it's been said, is in the eyes of the beholder."

She was in his face. In his space.

"I don't think you got that quite right," Martin said absently as his eyes took on the countenance of the beautiful young lady suddenly thrust upon him.

A vow of chastity made an enormous *whooshing* sound as it flew out the window. Their lips connected and within minutes Martin was no longer a holy man.

———

The first thing Martin saw in the morning was the hammered silver amulet. It nestled between a pair of the most beautiful breasts he had ever seen.

"Mmmm." Areeya stirred. Slowly she opened her eyes.

She looked at him for a moment, finally smiling and running a hand over the stubble of his hair.

"Hi."

He smiled, bent and kissed her perfect nipples.

———

It was late afternoon when Martin finally returned to his apartment. He had succumbed to a romantic interlude, and he didn't feel guilt. He had put all his other concerns away in their respective little boxes for a brief sweet moment. He could still taste her, still smell her, and he smiled as he crossed the dimly lit room.

All the boxes of his mind tumbled open when he saw the figure seated in the wicker lounge chair.

"What are you *doing* here?"

Lieutenant-Colonel Samarat didn't speak. He didn't smile. He just stared.

Martin pulled a drawstring and the bamboo slats allowed the afternoon sun into the room. Samarat squinted as he adjusted his eyes to the light. A bottle of Mekong whiskey was open on the table in front of him. It was half full.

"Where have you been?"

Martin sat in a matching chair opposite the cop. "None of *your* business."

"You're wrong. Everything you do is my business." He leaned forward. There was anger in his eyes. "I called you yesterday. I told you to meet me at seven. You ignored me."

He tossed something. A pair of handcuffs clattered onto the table in front of Martin. "Put them on."

Martin stared at the cuffs. "Don't be absurd—"

Samarat had drawn his 9-mm pistol and it was leveled at Martin's chest.

"Put them on."

Martin picked up the steel cuffs. He slipped them on his wrists. Slowly he ratcheted them closed. He sat back in his chair, his cuffed hands resting on his lap.

"Now what?"

"Now you tell me what you know. Where you've been. Where *he* is. No bullshit. No sorcerer's superstition crap, no garlic, black cats, or voodoo…just the facts. Tell me—" He moved the gun to Martin's face. "Tell me, or return to that little jailhouse crypt you're so fond of."

Martin cringed at the thought. He was terrified of spending another hour in the decrepit jail. But he was even more terrified of a drunken police officer with a loaded pistol. He tried to remain calm.

"Put the gun down…please."

Samarat slid the pistol back into his shoulder harness. He took a long pull on the whiskey bottle, wiping his lips with a folded handkerchief.

"Talk to me, Khun Larue."

"I saw him."

"I knew it."

"He's strong. Powerful. If anything he's more powerful than he was before."

Samarat seemed not to hear this. He was distracted by his own thoughts.

"The blind charlatan's dead, Khun Larue. You know that, don't you?"

"Charoen? No. I didn't. How?"

"His place was burned to the ground, him in it."

"How horrible."

"He didn't die in the fire. He had been bled dry."

"Lord." Martin shook his head.

"Don't act surprised. I'm sure he told you all about it."

"No. No he didn't. But he did say he was there when *we* met with Charoen. He was upstairs."

Samarat scowled. "Shit. What else?"

"You said there was another vampire?"

"Yes. We're finding bodies in Thonburi. It's rumored there's a female *phii dib*."

"I met her."

"You've been busy, Khun Larue." He toked on the whiskey bottle.

"She's responsible for bringing him back. Reincarnating him. In return, he gave her the gift."

"Some gift." Samarat sneered. "Who is she?"

"I don't know. She didn't tell me."

Samarat slammed his fist on the table. Martin reflexively raised his cuffed hands to his face.

"*Where is he?*"

"I don't know. That's the truth."

'But you *saw* him. Where?"

"At the cemetery."

"And you didn't tell me?"

"I didn't know he'd be there."

It was the truth, Martin reasoned. He really didn't know the vampire would be there.

Samarat slumped back in his chair, again lost in his own thoughts. "Listen, Khun Larue, whatever you did, whatever Boonsong did…there were others involved. Others aware of this, this…*thing*. But no one will talk about it. No one will talk to me."

He grabbed the bottle and finished it. He flung it and it smashed on the marble floor. He ignored it and stared straight at Martin. "To deal with this in a rational manner, I cannot…I *will not* accept your theories. This is a serial killer. A clinical *vampire*. A delirious man who believes he derives some strength from tasting the blood of his unfortunate victims."

Martin leaned forward. "That's bullshit. You know that's not true. *He's* a vampire. *She's* a vampire. Together they'll fill the Chao Phraya with bodies. They must be stopped."

The lieutenant-colonel stared blankly at Martin. There was no longer anger in his eyes. There was fear. His mouth was dry and the single word came out in a harsh whisper. "How?"

Mestaphel walked though the crowded market. Like the souks in his beloved homeland, the amount of merchandise was overwhelming. But unlike the bazaars of Afghanistan and their stalls of spices, oils, fruits, metals, religious ornaments, woven tapestries, and—more often than not— weapons of both western and eastern origin, this market consisted almost entirely of black-market copies of CDs and DVDs, and brand-name watches, clothes, accessories, and perfumes.

And pussy.

Patpong was truly the great decadent dream, Mestaphel concluded. The infidels finished their Big Macs at McDonald's and crossed the street to the 7-Eleven. Starbucks was a block away, but they would certainly close that gap soon. Outside the 7-Eleven they entered the demented Disneyland. Shops constructed of speed rail and rusty iron tables were crowded into one of two *sois*, quarter mile lanes crammed with the maximum per capita product to client exposure possible. Patpong seemed to be the single densest quarter-mile on the planet.

Introduced in the 60s for the sex-starved GIs of the Vietnam War, the street was lined on each side by two and three-story sex emporiums. Each ground floor held a go-go bar; the second floor was anything goes—vagina bazooka, ping-pong shooting, and skull fucking.

Perfect.

Mom and pop conned into a Southeast Asian cruise, couples who mistakenly believed Bangkok to be a typical tourist destination, and the ever present sex tourists—all strolled, or were pushed and shoved along in sardine-can formation. Sweaty body to sweaty body. Captive audience to the fourteen-year-old hawksters and *muay Thai*-trained punks who charmed, beguiled, and threatened them into buying the latest blockbuster movie, Grammy-winning CD, or diamond-studded Rolex.

Mestaphel strolled.

Mestaphel watched.

Mestaphel smiled.

Allah be praised. It was perfect.

He walked into a bar. Before him were dozens of teenage girls in white bikinis and cowboy boots. To his right and left were two tiers of cracked ruby vinyl booths. A sonic assault of mindless hip-hop rhythms boomed through distorted speakers.

Male tourists, Caucasian and Asian, all cavorted in various

stages of drunkenness with one, two, or more of the bikini-clad girls.

Perfect. He'd found his target. Intelligence had been correct. This was Ground Zero: American tourists shopping for trinkets. Infidels everywhere, frequenting corporate franchises. Decadent devils, pursuing their own double demons of alcohol and sex.

Oh the glory he'd receive. Oh the greatness of God.

The only question yet to solve was where to strike?

Maximum firepower. Maximum destruction.

He sat on a rickety barstool, wrapped an arm around a young girl in a string bikini, who stuck her tongue in his ear, ordered a double rum and coke, and pondered the questions.

16

Ramonne approached the bridge with caution. He was not sure of the state he would find her in. Martin had described her as very fragile, on the verge of suicide. His appearance would be a shock to her, even though she was waiting for him.

He would have gone to her earlier, but he'd had preparations to make. Certain acquisitions. Things one doesn't normally encounter. Research and investigation had occupied much of his time. But he needed to be ready for her.

He would do his best—his very best—not to fail her.

To save her. This was his goal.

He owed it to her.

When he finally saw her, he was amazed at how small she was. He realized that a week of not feeding had taken its toll. She was wasting away. Had she been human, she'd probably be dead—an irony that was not lost on him.

"Kanchana." He said the name softly, barely above a whisper.

She turned, startled, and he saw the ravaged face, still beautiful, but drawn and sunken. A contortion of what had been.

"*You*." She spat the word. "*Now* you come?"

He stepped onto the beam that spanned the twenty meters

that separated them. "I'm here for you. I came as soon as I could."

"Really? I've sat up here for a week, wailing like a banshee. *I know you heard me.* What took you so long?"

"Kanchana. I heard you, that's true. And yes, I did try to ignore you. I have my problems, also."

She hissed and wrapped her shawl tighter around her shoulders. The look she gave him was filled with venom. "You are strong. Stronger perhaps than before. You have no problems. You've been doing this for what? Two hundred years?"

"Not quite. But a long time, yes. I know what you're going through. I've been there. Right where you are."

"Bullshit."

"Kanchana. Trust me. I know. And I can help."

He held out his arms. She looked to him, her eyes moist dark pools. She started to get up. In an instant he had crossed the distance between them and helped her rise.

He took her in his arms and carried her off the bridge.

———

She slept. It was still night, and yet she slept. She was exhausted.

Ramonne brought her to the house on the *klong*. Loh, the faithful servant, had earlier made preparations for their arrival. A second coffin had been brought in for Ramonne, as he was not sure how many nights this would involve.

Loh ferried them from the bridge in the longtail boat and helped Ramonne carry the unconscious woman to her room. Ramonne laid her in her coffin and then utilized the remaining hours of darkness to his best advantage. When he finally crept into his guest coffin at dawn, he too was exhausted. He lay in the silk folds and pondered the steps that would be taken at the next nightfall.

He fell asleep uncertain of the outcome, but knowing that he would try to give her back the life he had only recently taken from her.

———

She woke to a room full of candles and strange smells. Scores of thick coils of incense burned, and charcoal soaked in fragrant oils glowed in metal braziers. The pungent smells wafted over her and heavenward. She attempted to sit up but was restrained.

Chains?

Her wrists and ankles were shackled. She suddenly felt the cold. She was chained to some sort of enormous marble slab.

"Ramonne?" she cried out.

"I'm here."

He appeared at her side and reached out to stroke her hair.

"Where am I?"

"You're in a graveyard."

She tugged at the chains. "Why am I chained?"

"What will happen will be repugnant to you. You will resist. I cannot allow that."

She looked at him with frightened, tired eyes. Eyes ready to embrace death. He felt it.

"You've lost hope. Long ago. Abandoned it. Yet, tonight, if you trust me...if you believe me...I can...I *will* give you what you long for." He spoke softly, gently.

"For three nights I have worked through a process of alchemy that the shaman taught me with his dying breath. I've experienced *nigredo*—the black phase—crushing, heating, dissolving certain substances under careful written calculation."

He held up a huge leather-bound book. Then he picked up a clear vial with a small amount of purple liquid.

"They've been broken down into their most primitive and base forms." He opened the sheer silk fabric that sheathed her body. She was nude beneath it.

He dipped two fingers into the vial and drew a line beneath her breasts and a long intersecting line from her throat to her pubic hair.

A cross.

"Then came the *citrinitas* or yellow phase. Bark of 400-year-old pine trees was procured and mixed with the blossom of a rare saguaro cactus."

He produced another vial. This one had a small spout. He leaned over Kanchana and kissed her softly before he poured the small amount of viscous liquid into her mouth. She swallowed without resistance.

"And finally the last phase...*rubedio*."

A breeze picked up and the smoke swirled around with his words. Fire rose and fell from the braziers.

"To move through these phases, the alchemist has to transcend the ordinary and achieve true vision. This I acquired through meditation and hallucination."

He looked to Kanchana, who now held him in awe.

"I am a destroyer, a magician, a seer. Now I have become a healer. The complex nature of my experience is denied to mere mortals. I recall being human...and I offer that—" He turned away from her and looked to the entry of the mausoleum. "To you."

He held out his hand. From the shadows, Loh emerged. By his side was a very young, very pale, naked girl.

Kanchana looked at the girl in horror. She knew...she could feel what was coming.

"No. I won't have it. Let me die—"

Ramonne put his hand up and she was silenced. His power was tremendous. "You cannot make this decision."

He motioned and the girl approached. She was obviously in a trance. He wrapped a protective arm around her and gently stroked her hair.

"This child is undeveloped. A mere babe. A virgin. Her potential in this life? A street child. Prostitution? A hapless marriage? Impoverished children? An untimely, ugly, early death?"

He held her close. Her doe-like eyes stared vacantly.

"She is so much more in the scenario *I* provide."

With that, he gently nudged her toward Kanchana.

"Ramonne. No. Please," Kanchana pleaded. "Let me die."

"No. I will let you live."

The girl mounted Kanchana and straddled her. She kissed each of her breasts and then writhed and moaned as she ground her pubescent vagina across the woman.

Ramonne reached out and grabbed onto the girl's long mane of hair. His eyes rolled back into his head as he looked skyward and uttered the final incantation.

"Just as, so they tell me, the sun rises every day in redness, so the ultimate enlightenment, the personal rebirth, the highest state of spiritual evolution, comes cloaked in red.

With that he drew his serrated knife and slit the girl's throat. Her life flowed from her and covered Kanchana in a red flood.

"Behold the 'Philosophers' Stone.'"

17

When the policeman finally departed, Martin remembered the remark made by the late charlatan. *Remain holy.*

Well, that option seemed to no longer be viable. He attempted to meditate to clear his thoughts, but he was unable to get *her* off his mind.

He picked up the phone.

"Hi."

She knew it was him before he said a word.

"Hi. Everything all right?"

"Yes. Except you're not here. I'm thinking of having a drink."

"Don't threaten me, Areeya. It won't work."

"Don't worry. I'm always *thinking* about having a drink...I won't."

"Good. That's my girl."

"Am I?"

"What?"

"Your girl."

Martin had to think about this.

"I guess you are."

"Good. I need a man in my life."

"Glad to be of service."

"Shut up, Martin. I'm serious."

"Sorry. Listen, I hate to change the subject, but Samarat was here when I got home."

"I'm not surprised. He's a cop. You stood him up."

"Yeah. He was pissed. Literally. He was drunk."

"Shit. What else did he do?"

"Not much. Mostly threats. Pulled his gun, though."

"Martin. Are you okay?"

"Of course. He's freaked out. Realizes he's got to deal with Ramonne, but can't bring himself to accept the truth."

"He has to. What's his plan?"

"That's what he asked me."

"That's crazy. Stay out of it."

"I can't. Samarat's never even met him. He has no idea what he's up against."

"I'll ask again. What's his plan?"

"I'll lead Samarat to the vampire. He'll arrest him."

"Arrest him? Is he insane?"

"That's all he's prepared to do. If he resists, he's preparing firepower to take him out."

"Firepower? Martin, I know what that monster is capable of. What it takes to stop him. I was with the two of you and Charoen. *He* warned him. Doesn't he have any idea—"

"No. No he doesn't. And Charoen's dead."

"That's terrible. I feel responsible."

"You're not. Anyway, Samarat refuses to believe the truth. But he does intend to do *something*. And if, God willing, the carnage isn't too terrible upon his first encounter with the vampire, he'll learn."

"So. That's the plan? Go blindly up against the beast. Lots of cops get killed…probably a few civilians. Lick your wounds and try again?"

"Maybe. Maybe I can figure something else out. But Samarat wants to start the hunt tonight. I'm leading the search."

"I'm going with you."

"No you're not."

"Martin, I know the truth. I know his power. You need my help. Besides, you forget…I'm protected."

"I'm not so sure about that. I have a feeling he humors it rather than fears it. He is getting stronger every day, every night. That talisman may soon have no effect."

"Martin, I don't think he'll harm you or me."

"He's a killer. He's not predictable. And he needs to be destroyed."

"You don't have to convince me. He killed my father. I want him to go back to hell. I want to help."

Martin was silent.

"Martin?"

"Do you want to drive?"

"Martin…your last girlfriend…she was your driver too, wasn't she?"

"What are you getting at? I don't drive—"

"Just don't think because you're rich, you can subjugate me."

"I…I—" Martin was speechless.

"Never mind. I'll pick you up at eight o' clock. But listen, don't tell anyone else you don't drive. It sounds way too gay."

With that she hung up and Martin sat there stunned, bewildered at how he had gone from celibate Buddhist to hen-pecked mate in the space of twelve hours.

Women.

She stirred. She moved a finger.

Ramonne allowed himself to breathe.

They were still in the graveyard. The incense smoldered and the braziers were dimmed. She was covered in blood. But even though almost eight hours had passed, the blood had not coagulated, and it appeared fresh, slick, and wet. Her whole body was painted with it.

This was crucial to the process. Immersion in a virgin's blood. He had gathered it as it ran off the stone she lay upon. Not a drop had been wasted. She had been bathed and rebathed in the virgin's blood.

"Necral baptism," the charlatan's book proclaimed.

He unlocked the cuffs and chains and wrapped her in white silk. He lifted her from the bier and carried her through the gates of the cemetery.

———

He bathed her in her large, gilded bathtub. He shampooed her long hair. After drying her, he brushed her hair and laid her on the fresh linens of her four-poster bed. Her pulse and temperature appeared normal. Her breathing was steady. The night sky was growing short, so he rose from her bedside. As a precaution he closed the shutters on her windows.

He left her room and went to the basement and his coffin.

It was midday when Kanchana woke. The room was dim and it took her a moment to realize she was not in her coffin. She felt the sheets. They were cool to her naked skin. She smelled her hair. It was clean and scented with lavender. She became aware of the small slivers of sunlight that played around the edges of the window shutters. There was a breeze blowing and a large branch was rattling outside the windows.

Cautiously she climbed out of the bed and crossed the room. The faint shafts of light came and went as the branch blew in the wind.

Nervously she approached the window. She extended a trembling hand to the sunbeams. She allowed a quarter-inch of light to graze her pale skin. She waited for it to burn.

It didn't.

She allowed the sun to move across her hand and up her arm. She held her breath and waited.

Nothing.

She unhooked the latch and flung the shutter wide open. The afternoon sun cascaded into the room, bathing her in the light.

She threw her head back and reveled in its luxurious warmth.

Tears flowed down her cheeks.

Tears of pure joy.

It was unbelievable, but undeniable.

She was reborn.

She was human.

———

Ramonne awoke just after dusk. As he rose from the coffin, he saw her.

She was seated in a chair next to the other, empty coffin. She was dressed in a simple light-blue dress, drawn in at the waist with a golden scarf. Next to her was a vase filled with fresh-cut flowers.

She was smiling.

"You've been out," he said.

"Yes. In the sun. It was wonderful."

He went and stood next to her. He smiled down at her. She extended her hand and he took it.

"Thank you."

He gently kissed her hand.

She looked up to his eyes. "I'm cured aren't I?"

"You're no longer a vampire. Yes."

"I know. But I mean I'm *cured*. I no longer have the disease. It's gone. I can feel it."

"Yes."

"That's amazing. There's hope for others now."

"I wouldn't suggest they follow your exact path."

Something *dark* flickered through her mind as Ramonne said this, and she flinched. Ramonne put a hand to her forehead. In a moment the dark thoughts were gone.

"It will take you a while to adjust. To forget."

————

Ping Narong lit a cigar as he watched Korn hang up the phone. As he did, he shook his head.

"I left the message again, Jao Phor. It is the third time in three days. He has not responded. Prichada has not seen him for over a week."

Ping puffed on the Monte Cristo and blew out a large, thoughtful plume of smoke.

"Find him."

18

Mestaphel had chosen his venue. The Music Café. Dead center of Patpong 1. The proper explosive device could level all of Patpong. The resulting fires and pandemonium, if done at the right time, would claim the lives of hundreds if not thousands.

But the size of the charge he needed was beyond the capacity of a suicide-bomber. It would require a vehicle. A car bomb. But this was a problem. After three o'clock in the afternoon, and again until six the following morning, the street was closed to traffic. The night market that was created took up every available inch of road and sidewalk, making it impossible to get even a motorbike through.

So a vehicle was ruled out. As an alternative, Mestaphel would simply divide up the explosive charges and strap them to three or four holy martyrs. The road to heaven was paved by such men. More volunteers would be easy to find. After all, who could resist the eternal reward: life in paradise surrounded by dozens of virgins.

Unfortunately, in Bangkok, the acquisition of martyrs for the cause was proving difficult. "Virgin *shmirgin*," he actually heard from one young man he approached. "Teenage whores are more than willing to sacrifice themselves to me. Why should I destroy my precious body?"

Mestaphel was not in the mood for this, and slit the coward's throat. "Let him be an example." Khun Yai proved an effective cleaner, and disposed of the body without undo comment or concern.

But the problem of the martyrs remained. Thailand's Muslim population was small, particularly in the north. The word went out to procure proper, respectful, diligent young men or women from the turbulent south, and send them north. As an added incentive their families would receive 50,000 baht in cash upon completion of their holy mission.

Mestaphel waited.

———

Ramonne smiled at Prichada as she opened his wine. "You've been away?" she asked.

"I've been...busy."

She smiled back as she poured a glass for him to taste. "They've been looking for you."

Ramonne shrugged. The matters of mortals were minor concerns to him. At best, he tolerated them. "They can wait."

Prichada looked to the rear of the restaurant. "Actually, these people don't like to wait. Korn's here."

Ramonne followed her eyes. He saw the spiky-haired, leather-clad punk. He turned back to Prichada, ignoring the youth.

"*He* can wait. How are you?"

She smiled again. This man was extraordinary. He had no fear. She made a decision to confide in him.

"I'd be better if I didn't have to work this stupid, deadend job."

He beat her to the punchline. "Eight hundred thousand baht...right?"

"What?"

"That's what it takes to open the beauty parlor you'd really like to run, instead of slinging fish heads and rice to arrogant assholes."

"How did you know?"

"Lucky guess."

The punk was approaching the table.

"You'll have it tomorrow."

"Excuse me?"

"I'll give you the money. I'll put it in an account in your name. The passbook will be yours tomorrow evening."

"Are you serious?"

"Of course."

"What do you want?"

"Only your happiness."

She stared, too shocked to speak.

Ramonne took her hand and gave it a gentle squeeze. It calmed her and she could breathe again. "Now. If you'll excuse me."

The young man sat down opposite Ramonne. "Singha," he snapped at Prichada.

She didn't hear it. Didn't even see him.

"Singha! *Yai!*" he snapped again. Then "Bitch" under his breath.

Like lightning, Ramonne pushed the table into the young man so violently and with such force that his breath and blood flow were cut off. His eyes bulged as he realized he was a step away from death.

"Apologize. Apologize or die."

"I...I'm sorry."

Ramonne relaxed his leverage and Korn caught his breath. Prichada stared in shock. Ramonne made a motion with his hand, which assured her that she should just leave. She bowed lightly and faded away.

"So. Why are you here?"

The young gangster mopped his brow, which was covered in sweat. "Ping has been seeking you."

"And?"

"That should be enough."

"It isn't."

Korn mulled this for a moment, and then leaned in. He spoke in a whisper. "He told me to tell you he has wind of a planned Muslim terrorist attack on Bangkok."

Muslims. Ramonne pondered the term. He had dismissed all religion as a whole as having played a minor role if any in his existence. Certainly, if there was a God, then Ramonne was damned. In general he thought their organized practice did more harm than good. He had little tolerance for their hypocritical ways. He was not surprised that the words

'Muslim' and 'terrorist' seemed synonymous these days.

"And?"

"And he wants you to intervene. This would be terrible for business."

"There is a price for this?"

"Of course."

"Then let's go see Ping."

Ramonne downed his wine and stood. Korn had trouble getting out of his seat, and Ramonne had to help him to his feet.

——————

The photographs were grainy, shot with a long lens from across a crowded street or from a second-floor window. They showed a bearded man meeting with other bearded men.

"Which one do I kill?" Ramonne asked as he handed
Ping the pictures.

"Kill them all if you can." Ping snorted in disgust. "Can you imagine the nerve? Just waltz into *my* town and decide to blow it up. I ask you, what did we ever do to them?"

Ramonne knew the question wasn't aimed at him, but he shrugged anyway. "Why Bangkok?"

"Why not? Seems these towel-heads have access through the border to Malaysia. They can pass into Thailand without causing red lights to go off. Here, they can get anything they need. That's how I found out about this. They're buying explosives, lots of them, and stockpiling it in our warehouses in Klong Toey docks."

"Where and when is the hit?"

"Don't know. We got what we do know from a driver who has a taste for opium. Unfortunately, he died."

Ramonne didn't ask.

"It is probably soon," Ping said. "Our guess is that they're building a car bomb. Probably like the job they pulled in Bali."

"Then they're after a tourist target."

"No doubt. And no doubt someplace I have an interest in. And no doubt it will be bad for business. *My* business."

"For a moment there, I thought you had a humanitarian streak." Ramonne smirked.

"I don't give a fuck if these assholes want to blow up other towel-heads. I don't give a fuck if they want to fight wars over shitty barren deserts. But stay the fuck out of my business. Stay the fuck out of my town."

He tapped one of the bearded men in the photos.

"This fuck. This is the big snakehead. Him I want dead. *Now*."

Ramonne studied Mestaphel's face, committing it to memory.

"And the price?"

"Ten million baht."

Ramonne smiled.

"It shall be done."

———

They came.

He was amazed at how young they were. Wide-eyed and innocent. But ready to die. They would do this for Allah and their families. And, of course, the virgins.

Within a week there were half-a-dozen youths sequestered in a safe house. Mestaphel thoroughly tested their mettle. Two he reduced to tears within the first day and sent back to their mothers. He also informed their local *mullah* and knew the boys would suffer untold indignities. The other six seemed worthy.

But they were children. Teenagers. He was asking them to go into the infidels' playground unnoticed. Each wearing twenty pounds of explosives. The timers would be remotely detonated. He couldn't leave that up to the children. They'd learned this through experience. Volunteers could become terrified when the moment of glory came, and flee the scene like drunken lorry drivers involved in a collision.

How to get them into the area, to Ground Zero, without arousing suspicion?

Patpong, as loose and wild as it appeared, was in fact tightly controlled—at least on the surface. The police maintained checkpoints at both the Silom and Surawong Road entrances. A mobile unit was prominently stationed at each end to discourage pickpockets and muggers, and random patrols of jack-booted officers on 'social order' duty swept the area and maintained a surreal façade of order. Real or imaginary threat, the mere presence of the authorities caused Mestaphel to be very precise in his planning.

If one of the boys were detained upon entry, the whole plan would be exposed, and the ripples it would cause would be devastating to the entire *jihad*.

This was totally, absolutely unacceptable.

19

Martin looked in the mirror. He figured he had about a minute before Areeya would be ringing his doorbell. She had called from the lobby and he had buzzed her up. As he checked his appearance, he realized he hadn't had a visitor to the apartment other than Samarat in over a year. Since Daeng left.

Daeng.

He didn't often think about her, but when he did, it was with a depressing sense of loss. And unanswered questions. *Why? What happened?* Well, actually, that was fairly clear. Unlike other relationships, that suffer tensions, tests, and stress, theirs had been interrupted by the appearance of a vampire. One who had tortured and demonized Martin so that he had virtually lost his humanity. This was what stretched their relationship to the breaking point.

Martin picked up a hairbrush. Hers. It was small. Almost child-like. He held it, when the doorbell buzzed.

He opened the door.

"Hi."

"Hi."

They both stood there.

"Are you going to invite me in?"

"Yes. Yes, of course. Come in."

She strolled through the apartment, taking it in.

"Very nice." She noticed that every table had stacks of books. "You read a lot?"

"Yes. It comes with having too much idle time."

The phone rang.

"Excuse me." He picked up the cordless in the hall.

"Yes?"

He listened a minute and then simply said "Yes" again and hung up.

"Samarat?"

He nodded. "He wants to start the hunt tonight. We're meeting at the bridge at ten."

Areeya checked her watch. "That gives us two hours." She started unbuttoning her blouse. "Plenty of time."

Martin took her in his arms and they sank into the folds of a leather couch.

———

Areeya's blue BMW was waved through the checkpoint that had been set up on the bridge. A convoy of police vehicles, their red lights swirling, lined the road, and the bridge was closed to traffic. A hook and ladder fire truck was being parked at the bottom of one of the huge stanchions that supported the bridge.

They could go no further, so Areeya parked. Two uniformed cops escorted them to Samarat. He was barking orders into a walkie-talkie. He handed the radio to Manat when he saw Martin.

"How kind of you to join us."

Martin nodded. "Why the circus?"

"I'll explain in a moment. Tell me about the other...vampire."

"I came out here, drawn by a wailing cry that I had been hearing for two nights. I finally followed it to its source."

"When was that?"

"Four nights ago."

"Sergeant. Are you aware of any noise complaints to match this…*wailing*?"

"No, sir. It may have been a boat motor or—"

Martin raised his hand. "It wasn't. I believe that other than Ramonne, who the cry was intended for, I may be the only person to hear it."

Lieutenant-Colonel Samarat rolled his eyes and Manat gave a slight smirk.

"Go on, Khun Larue."

While they talked, the giant ladder from the fire truck was swung into position and started to slowly ascend up the side of the stanchion. Two firemen were lashed to the top of the ladder.

"She told me that she had been made a vampire by Ramonne. She had knowledge of how he'd been reborn, and implicated Charoen as having masterminded the resurrection." Martin saw no need to go into details.

"This vampire didn't attack you?"

"No. She didn't. She knew who I was and told me that she wanted to die. She was waiting for Ramonne to come to her, but if he didn't, then she would wait for the sun and incinerate herself."

"I thought that could only happen on holy ground?"

Another smile was exchanged between Samarat and Manat.

"The young, the recently turned, are nowhere near as strong as the old. They are very vulnerable to fire and sunlight."

Martin looked at the network of cables that held the bridge. All appeared empty.

"He must have taken her away."

Samarat handed Martin a powerful pair of field binoculars. "Perhaps not." He pointed to the top of the stanchion where the ladder was making its slow ascent.

Martin raised the glasses and adjusted the focus.

"Lord."

There was a small platform twenty feet from the top. A figure was seated there. It had long hair, but it was impossible to make out any more details, except that it appeared to be dead. It did not move.

The ladder had almost completed its ascent. Samarat took the handset again and talked to one of the firemen.

Martin watched through the binoculars as they approached the platform.

"Well?" Samarat demanded.

"It's a woman. She's dead."

Martin watched as one of the firemen attempted to brush the hair away from the face. As soon as he touched it, the woman's head fell onto the platform. "Good Lord."

"What is it?" Samarat squinted up at the scene above.

"She's been burned." The fireman attempted to move the torso and it collapsed into a pile of ash and bones.

A body bag was lifted out of a box on the ladder, and the two men carefully put the charred pieces of the woman into the bag. As they did, they became aware of the rope that had lashed her to the stanchion.

"This is impossible."

"What now!" Colonel Samarat was getting increasingly frustrated.

"I'm assuming she committed suicide, climbed up here, lashed herself to the pole, and doused herself with gas. But the rope...it's not burned. Not even touched by fire."

Samarat looked at Martin, who had a protective arm around Yaya. Thankfully she had not seen anything, only heard the exchange.

Martin handed the glasses to Manat. "I guess he never came for her after all."

The body bag was lashed to the ladder and it started to descend.

Martin thought that somewhere, far in the distance, he heard a cry. That dreadful sound.

He didn't mention it.

———

Ramonne motioned to Loh, and he untied the line that held the longtail boat to the dock. Two pulls and the motor roared to life.

They headed north, away from the Rama III Bridge. Ramonne's keen vision was still able to make out the firemen as they opened the body bag and Samarat peered within. The colonel made no more than a cursory glance and then ordered the bag sealed.

This was Ramonne's final gift to Kanchana.

He'd carried the lifeless form of the sacrificial young girl to the top of the bridge and set her on fire. When he was satisfied that the corpse was still recognizable as female, but unidentifiable, he extinguished the fire and lashed her in place.

Now Kanchana could return to life in peace, free from the fear of police intrusion. He knew the Bangrak constabulary well, and was confident the case of the female vampire was now closed.

20

He had no name. No address. He was a shadow.

Ramonne began to admire the terrorist's knack for being invisible. Ramonne should know. He'd remained virtually invisible for 140 years.

There had, indeed, been a huge cache of explosives stored in one of Ping's Klong Toey warehouses. But before Ramonne could be contacted, it had vanished. All traces removed in the middle of the night. The only thing Ramonne had to go on were the photographs. He committed them to memory and then burned them.

One opportunity not open for Ramonne was the fact that the man would no doubt be praying regularly, somewhere. But that would be during the day.

Ramonne, however, had the advantage of 140 years spent studying human nature. He'd picked up more than a little insight. He knew various people's habits. He could tell you where a good German would have his first beer in Nana Plaza fifteen minutes after he checked into his Sukhumvit hotel room. If a Brit was a bit cultured, he'd make his way to the Foreign Correspondent's Club or the Siam Society for their weekly events. Belgians and Americans favored the trendy Q Bar, while

Italians and French headed straight for the beaches of Phuket and Koh Samui.

The Muslims, however, now they were—he hated to use modern slang, but it fit—kinky. They came to Thailand *sans* baggage. No wives. They came to indulge. Just like the foreign workers who toiled on their oil rigs and endured sixty days of doing without alcohol and women, the Muslims crammed a lifetime of abstinence into a week in Thailand. He knew the few brothels where devout Muslims shook off the dust of their existence in some desert and debauched and indulged until they retched their guts out. He'd found them easy prey. He'd catch them as they wandered into the alleys looking for a place to relieve their bloated bladders.

In their attempts to cram as much sexual relief as possible into a relatively short period of time, they tended to frequent those dens of iniquity that seemed to stretch the limits of depravation even by Bangkok standards. Ramonne dove into the quest with relish. He visited bondage parlors, dominatrixes, torture chambers, and straight-sex bordellos where men had sex with seven women at a time. At times, even Ramonne's acute vision had trouble making out exactly what was going on. He met pimps and gimps, geeks and freaks, firemen, doctors, lawyers, Indian chiefs…and yet the mystery terrorist remained unseen.

All the while, he kept his vampire radar sharply tuned, for he knew they were looking for him. He knew that Samarat and Bangrak's finest were on his trail.

And he knew Martin was with them.

He felt fairly confidant, the deeper he plunged into the city's nefarious depths, that he was making it more difficult for his hunters. Martin had never been down these paths, and wouldn't know where to lead them.

Or so he thought.

"Anything…Khun Larue?"

The handset squawked and Martin jumped. He'd forgotten that Samarat had handed it to them before they left the Bangrak Police Station.

He picked it up.

"Nothing…Over." He felt like an idiot, using the thing.

Areeya smiled. "Martin. I think you have to squeeze the button on the side when you talk."

"Oh yeah." He squeezed. "Nothing."

He released the button and Samarat squawked again.

"Where are you taking us?"

"I don't really know. I found him last time by just following what I thought were my instincts. But he told me I followed something else. That we were connected, and that if I chose to let it happen, I'd be drawn to him."

Martin paused, still holding the button.

"That's what I'm trying to do. Over."

They drove in silence. Samarat was in a plain white sedan, three car lengths behind. Two well stocked police trucks followed close behind. They had tear gas, riot guns, machine guns, the works.

Martin knew the firepower would have little effect, but hoped that at least the sheer volume might stun Ramonne enough for them to cart him off to hallowed ground and extinction.

Again.

But that would only be if he could convince Samarat, who was still of a mind to attempt an arrest. Martin figured that actually seeing the vampire in action might allow saner judgment to prevail.

They drove along Sukhumvit, turning into Soi 13. As Areeya's car passed the Gardens of Babylon, the handset barked.

"Pull over," Samarat ordered.

Sergeant Manat exited the police car and entered the club. In a few minutes he was back, shaking his head.

"Well?" Areeya turned to Martin and he had a sense of *déjà vu*, remembering back to the night that Daeng had driven he and Jonathan through the city night in a similar quest for the vampire.

"Head for Klong Toey."

She did. The cops were in tow.

———

Within thirty minutes they were stopped in the warehouse row alongside a massive pier.

"Drive slowly. And turn off your lights."

"Turn off my lights? Why?"

"I don't know. Just do it, please."

They cruised past row upon row of enormous warehouses. Most had a sodium vapor lamp illuminating their huge doors. They were all locked tight.

All but one. Its doors were open. The light above was extinguished.

"Stop."

Martin got out of the car. He looked into the cavernous space. It was pitch black within. He started to enter when suddenly a white flash of light nearly blinded him. In the instant of the strobe-flash he saw a silhouette.

He leaped back, falling over a piece of broken pipe and landing on his ample butt.

"Martin? What happened? Are you okay?"

Martin scrambled to his feet, shaken. "Yeah. I'm all right. Did you see that?"

"See what?"

"The light. It flashed like a strobe."

"No. I didn't."

Martin looked back at the warehouse. Samarat and Manat were now at his side. Manat had a large flashlight.

Martin repeated himself: "There was a light, and someone was there."

Samarat motioned and Manat and a half-dozen officers entered the warehouse, guns drawn and flashlights sweeping their powerful beams into every corner.

It was completely empty. Bare.

"Nothing." Manat turned off his light.

Instantly, Martin saw another flash and the figure again. This time it was departing. In a split second it was gone.

"What was that?" Martin blurted out.

"What was *what*?" Samarat asked.

"That flash. Didn't you see *that*?"

"Martin." Areeya looked at him, scared. "There was nothing."

"I saw another flash and a figure. It was Ramonne…I'm sure. He was leaving."

"Martin. You're seeing things."

He moved to the doorway and looked back at the empty pier beyond them.

"Yes. I am. It's not the first time."

"Make sure of what you saw, Khun Larue."

"He *was* here."

"You said that before. You said he often comes here."

"No. I mean recently. Maybe 24 hours. I don't know. But I think that now I can *see* where he's *been*."

———

Mestaphel surveyed the room. Boxes, metal canisters, ice coolers, PVC pipe, wire, backpacks, oxygen tanks, torches, aluminum foil. All fairly innocuous. He carefully lifted a heavy canvas tarp. Underneath were the real tools of his trade: Nitric and sulfuric acid, glycerin, sodium bicarbonate, potassium permanganate, iodine crystal, magnesium powder, packets of ammonium nitrate with oil fillings, kerosene, black powder, sulfur, carbon, blasting caps, petroleum jelly, duct tape, and electric fuses.

He knew where.

He knew how.

And he knew *who*. There were just four boys now. Two more had been weeded out. One was caught 'boasting' of his bravery in a coffee shop. Thank Allah he gave no details, but the owner, a Jamah Islamiyah cell member, was quick to report him. The boy suffered the indignity of having his tongue cut out, before his throat was slit.

The other boy was just too dark, too Arab looking to pass through the zone unchallenged.

There would be a gauntlet of sorts to pass through before the deed could be done. It included the police checkpoints—not really enforced or well manned, but more of a visual presence in the area. The boys needed to be innocuous, innocent looking, invisible.

They would travel to the zone together, in a rented van. The first two boys, Hasheem and Kahlid, would be dropped off on Surawong Road at the Tawana Ramada Hotel. They would go into the coffee shop and join an adult operative who would 'monitor' their attitude. The van would proceed down Narathivat Road and back up Silom. Mestaphel himself would stay with the other two boys, Abdul and Omar. He would be their monitor.

The van would pull into the hospital loading zone a block before the entry to Patpong, and Mestaphel would call the operative at the Tawana. This would be the signal for them to move. They would slowly walk along Surawong, past the entry to Patpong 1, and on down the street to Patpong 2. Here, under the garish "Pink Panther A-Go-Go" sign, the adult operative would leave the boys. He would continue on down the street while the boys walked into the zone, past restaurants and beer bars.

Mestaphel would accompany his two children. He would also lead them past the main tourist entry point to the *gai yang* vendors and luggage stalls that crowded the southern entry to Patpong 2. Here he was confident the boys would encounter no interference as they made their way up the *soi*. He would lead them as far as the multi-tiered car park.

They were then to go to Foodland, where they would find the first two young martyrs in the canned goods aisle. Without acknowledging each other, they would proceed to the checkout, purchasing small items—chewing gum, orange soda. They would smoke a cigarette and wait outside for the first two boys to depart.

At five minutes to midnight they would walk to the Music Café.

It would take less than a minute.

Upon entering they would seek their positions. One in each corner of the entry. Abdul and Omar would already be deep in the club.

Four boys, each with twenty pounds of explosives either strapped to their body or in school backpacks.

At exactly midnight, four cellphones would ring, and four of God's chosen one's would ascend straight to heaven.

Hundreds of infidels would descend to hell.

God is great.

Mestaphel monitored the moisture content on several of the bomb components. Satisfied, he replaced the tarp and locked the heavy metal door.

He knew where.

He knew how.

He knew *when.*

21

Two men drank together and talked of the problems of the world. Strangers, they shared the common bond that a barstool and a shot glass provide. It was a scene repeated every night in every city, town, and hamlet around the globe. The only differ ence was that this bar was in a notorious brothel in Bangkok, and one man was a terrorist and the other was a vampire.

"You're French…yes?"

Ramonne nodded.

"Good. Your people were right to stand up to the Americans."

Mestaphel raised his glass in salute. Ramonne half-heartedly raised his wine glass.

It had been a stroke of pure luck that had placed him in the bar of the Gull's Nest. He knew its reputation for underaged girls drew a rather seedy crowd, but as to how many of the pedophiles were Muslim, he had no idea. He asked the bartender and was told that *yes*, there was a Muslim guest upstairs with a couple of girls. Ramonne had ordered a bottle of wine and decided to wait. Within half an hour, the man came down the stairs. It was Mestaphel.

Instead of leaving, however, the Muslim sat down and ordered a whiskey.

It was late and there were just the two of them at the bar.

The man was very drunk. He drank in silence while Ramonne read his thoughts.

Mestaphel used the girls to rid himself of the pent-up anxiety he had been feeling. He used the whiskey to clear his head and run through the plan one more time.

Ramonne *saw* the preparation of the bombs, the mixing of the two acids with the glycerin, the forming and separation of the nitroglycerin. The careful pouring into canisters. These were then taped to plastic pipe sections filled with black powder. Small blasting caps were inserted, and these were attached to electrical fuses. The whole thing was loaded into a backpack and strapped onto a youth.

Ramonne *saw* all of this and it terrified him, for next he saw that same boy walking through a crowded Patpong.

Ramonne squeezed his wineglass with such force that it shattered.

This brought the man out of his stupor and he stared at Ramonne.

Ramonne swept the glass aside and the bartender brought another.

"Are you all right?" the Muslim asked.

"Yes. I'm fine. I just had a disturbing thought. *Comme si, comme sa.* It doesn't matter."

"You're French...yes?"

And so a dialogue began between the two men. A hate-filled conversation that Ramonne soon grew weary of. It was too full of racial prejudice and vitriol, and Ramonne wanted to rip the man's throat out. But the image of the boy with the explosive pack wandering his beloved Patpong unnerved him. He had to make sure that it did not happen. And killing this degenerate would not guarantee that. He had to know more.

"Your views are very interesting. But I'm afraid I must depart."

He finished his wine and pushed his stool away from the bar.

Mestaphel nodded and returned to his whiskey. The last thought Ramonne read before he left the bar was, *Stinking French scum.*

Ramonne vowed that this man's death would not be pleasant.

———

Ramonne waited on the roof for the man to leave. It was another hour, and the bartender had to help the man get through the door. The neon sign of the whorehouse bar sputtered and went dark. The man staggered down the street.

It was easy for Ramonne to follow him. Mestaphel was so drunk that he was not aware of his surroundings. Ramonne stayed about twenty feet behind, unable to read his drunken, incoherent thoughts.

Within thirty minutes the man stumbled through the lobby of the Lux. Ramonne watched him get into the elevator and saw a third-floor light come on in a corner room. Minutes later the light was extinguished.

———

Kanchana woke with a start. She was not alone.

"Don't be afraid," Ramonne whispered.

She sat up in her bed and ran a hand through her hair.

"I'm not. Just surprised. Why are you here?"

"I have an errand for Loh. And I wanted to see you."

He moved to the bedside and sat next to her. He took her hand, gently. He checked her pulse. "How are you feeling?"

"Fine. But I still have trouble sleeping at night. It's a little like jet lag."

He smiled.

"What do you need from Loh?"

"I need him to follow someone. I wrote the details down." He withdrew a parchment envelope and placed it on the table.

She lightly caressed his hand. "You know that amulet he wears?"

"Yes."

"He offered it to me today. I told him I don't need it."

"You don't."

"I know. But, I have to ask…Does *he*?"

"No."

"I didn't think so."

She looked up at his eyes. His mane of hair with its single silver streak was back-lit by the moonlight through the windows. She reached up and stroked his cheek.

"Do you think that we—"

"No." He knew what she was thinking. "It is far too dangerous. I fear I would not be able to control myself."

"I know I could not control *myself*."

He smiled. "You know what I mean."

She sighed. She did.

"You are beautiful. You'll find love. You have time."

"Thanks to you." She took his hand and kissed it.

He leaned over and kissed her on the forehead. He passed a hand over her eyes and in an instant she was deep asleep.

22

They met at the Rachinee Pier. It was opposite the mouth of Klong Bangkok Yai, and Loh used that canal to travel to and from Thonburi. The vampire sat at a table and watched the river traffic. Behind him, steam from boiling prawns floated over the Christmas lights that decorated the little restaurant. Loh arrived precisely at the appointed hour. Ramonne liked this about the man. He was punctual, trustworthy, and reliable. He called to the girl and Loh ordered a tall Singha beer.

"He is a very bad man, master."

"I know that, Loh. What did you see."

Loh told how he had staked out the coffee shop. Mestaphel had made his appearance around noon. He was obviously hungover and in a foul mood. He barked at the waitress for not bringing his coffee fast enough. He made two cellphone calls, glanced quickly through the *Bangkok Times*, and checked his watch repeatedly. Within half an hour, a second burly Muslim appeared, driving a Volvo sedan. Mestaphel was angry, as the man was obviously late, and hit him repeatedly about the head with the rolled up newspaper, all the way to the car. Loh had earlier secured a taxi driver, who was waiting outside. They followed the Volvo.

It drove northward until it pulled into a parking lot along-side the Chatuchak Weekend Market. The driver stayed with the car while the other man walked into the labyrinth that on weekends would be swelled to bursting with buyers and sellers of everything under the sun. Loh had a few anxious minutes as he lost sight of the man in the time it took to exit the taxi. But the weekend had yet to arrive and the market was virtually empty and he was soon in sight.

Mestaphel made his way to a row of godowns in the rear of the market. A bearded man stood outside, smoking. He had put out the cigarette when Mestaphel approached. He straightened his posture and almost saluted. Mestaphel ignored him and went into the building. The man had shut the door behind him and taken out another cigarette.

Loh gulped his beer at this point, becoming excited.

"And then?"

"Then I went to the back of the building, hoping there would be an unguarded rear entrance."

"Yes?"

"Unfortunately there was a guard at the rear, also. Master, you told me to do what I had to do to get the information you desire."

"I did. What did you do?"

"I...I asked the man for a light, and when he reached for his lighter I slit his throat."

This caused Ramonne to pause.

"Did anyone see you?"

"No, master. And I dragged the body into the swamp grass."

Ramonne shook his head slightly. Loh never failed to surprise him.

"Go on."

Loh had then slipped into the rear of the warehouse and quietly climbed a wooden staircase to a second-floor gantry. He crawled on his stomach until he was directly over the center of the room. He strained to see what was happening.

Below him, several bearded men carefully loaded powder and liquids into small sections of blue PVC pipe. Mestaphel sat on an overturned barrel and four teenage boys sat on the floor in front of him.

"*Four?*"

"Yes, master."

Ramonne seethed as he thought of the evil this man intended.

"The one you seek talked in a language I do not understand. A Muslim dialect of some sort. But it was obvious the boys were his willing slaves. They seemed under his spell. After a while he had them try on the backpacks after they were loaded with the bombs. Two had the packs, and two had vests with the bombs attached. After they seemed accustomed to the weight and some adjustments were made, they were carefully removed."

As Loh told the tale, Ramonne pictured it in his mind. He *saw* the boys' faces, the trembling excitement as they first felt the weight of the explosives. They smiled. *They actually smiled.*

"When this was done, he took each boy alone and embraced him. He kissed them on the head and said the same word to each. This word I understood."

"What did he say?"

"*Tomorrow.*"

Ramonne pondered this.

It gave him time. Time to plan.

"And then, master, I slithered back down the stairs and left before I could be discovered."

Ramonne smiled. "You did well, Loh." Ramonne handed over an envelope stuffed with baht. The servant took it gratefully and *waied* deeply.

"Meet me again at midnight. Arrange to have a car and take me to his warehouse. First we will destroy his tools, and then I will deal with the devil himself."

"Yes, master."

Ramonne got up and left the ramshackle restaurant via the kitchen.

Loh finished his beer and counted his money. He stuffed the envelope into his pocket and walked to the pier. He was untying the boat when he became aware of footsteps on the planks behind him. He turned and was surprised to see the taxi driver who had driven him throughout the day.

"You're still here?"

Loh remembered Ramonne's request for a car later tonight, so perhaps this was fortunate. He stood to talk to the man when he suddenly felt a wire around his neck. He clawed at the wire, but it was already cutting into his throat, cutting off his oxygen. He struggled, but the iron grip was too powerful. Soon he collapsed and died.

The hands released the grip on the wire and Loh's body fell to the ground. One hand went into his pocket and took the envelope of cash. Another tore the silver amulet from Loh's neck. The body was kicked into the river.

Mestaphel watched it float among the drifting garbage and then turned to the taxi driver. The terrorist handed the envelope of money to the man and walked away.

———

Martin saw the *flash*.

"Stop."

In front of McDonald's at the base of CP Tower, Martin had *seen* the image of the vampire standing on the steps scanning the crowd. He got out of the car. He looked back across Silom Road. He saw another flash…the vampire crossing the street.

"There." He pointed.

Areeya left her car at the curb, amidst the curses of a half-dozen *tuk-tuk* drivers, and followed Martin into the street.

Samarat and his militia pulled into the car park entry and stopped. They scrambled to catch up with Martin.

Martin paused at the entry to Patpong 2. He looked up and down Silom.

Nothing.

He looked down the narrow alley. Another *flash*. Another figure.

He charged into the *soi*. Midway he became confused. Overwhelmed. "We're close to him. He's…he's everywhere."

He saw flashes of Ramonne in every direction he looked. Sitting outside Cosmos chatting with the girls. In a window seat at Caffé di Roma sipping his wine. Stuffing a body into a water tank above the carpark.

"He must live here. Somewhere." Martin shook his head and plunged on, Colonel Samarat and his small army right behind.

The parade of armed cops was viewed with little concern by the denizens of Patpong. Jack-booted raids, random urine tests, were part of the new social order and were nothing unusual. They were generally regarded as a nuisance, nothing to be alarmed about.

Martin stopped just past the Star of Love bar. He looked at a door. He *saw* Ramonne entering.

"I think this is where he lives."

He touched the doorknob and it shocked him like 100 watts of electricity. He pulled his hand back.

Samarat motioned and two officers opened the door, their guns extended before them.

The entry was empty.

They stepped back and Martin entered. Immediately he saw a flash of Ramonne at the elevator. He started up the stairs, Samarat and the troops following. Areeya elected to stay downstairs.

They made it to the top floor without incident. A single door stood before them.

"There." Martin stood back as two officers approached. They looked to Samarat for a signal. He nodded and, in unison, they kicked the door. It flew off its hinges into the room. The cops flattened themselves against the doorway. They'd been trained to expect gunfire. Martin knew that would never come.

No. It will be worse.

After a moment of silence they cautiously entered the room. Martin held his breath.

One minute. Two minutes passed.

Then one of them appeared in the doorway.

"It's empty."

Samarat stepped into the room.

"Colonel." It was the second officer. He was in the rear of the long and narrow room. An alcove had been created with a beaded curtain as a room divider. Samarat walked through the curtain to the officer.

He was standing in front of an ornate mahogany coffin.

"Lord Buddah."

The lid was closed. Samarat drew his pistol and motioned to the officer. Carefully, holding his AK-47 with one hand, he lifted the lid.

Time seemed to stand still.

"Empty."

Samarat stared at the silken interior and re-holstered his gun.

———

A lone policeman stayed with Areeya at the entry to the apartment building. She wanted a cigarette. She wanted a drink…Hell, she wanted to smoke crack.

Two nights of vampire chasing and she was folding…caving in. And Martin? He'd gone right over the top. He was seeing things. Things that not only were not there now, but things that *used* to be there. He'd taken to hanging his head out the car window like a dog and then screaming out "stop" when something appeared on his radar screen. She'd slam on the brakes and he'd stare at nothing. An empty street. A vacant lot. A doorway. And he'd be more and more excited each time. "Yes," he'd shout out. "He was here. Not long ago." He'd assure Samarat they were getting closer. Samarat would roll his eyes and away they'd go…again.

Cops. She'd grown up with them. They'd been following her ever since she became a teenager. Following on Daddy's orders. Following to make sure she stayed out of trouble.

And now they were following her again.

"Hey."

Martin appeared.

"Hey. What's happening?"

"We found his lair. His home."

She shuddered. She remembered his prior dwelling place. She'd been his unwilling guest.

"He's not there."

"I gathered that. What's Samarat doing?"

"Searching the place. Looking for evidence."

"Was there a coffin?"

"Yes."

She shuddered again. "What more evidence does he need?"

"I don't know. Let's take a walk. His presence is overwhelming."

They moved down the *soi*. The cop stayed in the doorway.

Martin was sweating. He kept blinking.

"Martin. What's wrong?"

"I keep seeing him. Everywhere. And then he's gone."

Now Martin saw the vampire right in front of them. He blinked.

He is still there.

"Hello boy."

Areeya shrieked.

"Lord. It's you."

"Of course it's me. Who did you expect?"

Areeya started to scream. Ramonne clamped a strong hand over her mouth.

"Sorry."

His forearm brushed the amulet and he pulled away as if he'd been burned. He looked at the skin, puzzled.

Areeya clutched the amulet. "Don't you come near me."

"Don't worry. I won't. What *is* it with that thing?"

Areeya was shaking. She started to scream again.

"Areeya. Don't." This time it was Martin's hand over her mouth.

"Thank you," Ramonne offered. "So, you brought the coppers, eh boy."

"You knew I would."

"What will they do?"

"I don't know. I don't think they know. They're not really convinced you're not human."

"Well, I can take care of that little problem. But unfortunately, you've caught me at a bad time. I'm a little busy right now."

"I don't think there's going to be a choice. Samarat's ready for a confrontation. Now."

"He'll just have to wait. Ramonne looked at Martin. His eyes burned into him. "Martin. How did you find me?"

"I...I suppose I tracked you. I was able to see where you'd been."

"As I suspected, we have a kinetic bond. I don't know how. I don't know why. But I'm learning. Remember the woman?"

How could he forget.

"She's not dead, Martin. I saved her. I cured her."

"I saw her body—"

"No. No you didn't. You saw what I wanted you and the police to see." Ramonne smiled. "Do you understand? After 140 years, I'm finally learning why I'm the way I am. Why I'm here. I'm finally in touch with...aware of...my destiny."

"I don't understand."

"Nor do I. Not fully. But I think that just perhaps...just possibly...instead of being the decimator of mankind's unwanted, instead of being a nefarious nightstalker, I just might possibly have a purpose."

Martin stared. Dumbfounded. Astonished. He was listening to a vampire defend his role in life.

"You told me you were a hit man?"

"*That*? That's just a job. But I do it well."

"That's sick."

Areeya was backing down the alley, trying to get away from the madness.

"Martin. That's actually where it all started. Where I saw I could do some good. Provide a service."

Lord. Martin sighed. *This is definitely the end of the world.*

Areeya slipped past the Cozy Club and ran. Neither

Martin nor Ramonne noticed she was gone.

"Listen. I know you want to bring me down…and I understand that. I really do. But tonight is *not* a good night. If you knew what was really going on."

"Try me."

"Really?"

"Yes. Tell me."

This had never occurred to Ramonne, but hell, it was worth a try.

"I've been hired to kill a terrorist who's going to set off bombs in Bangkok. Here. In Patpong. Tomorrow night."

"You're serious?"

"Martin. You of all people should know not to question me."

"When?"

"Tomorrow. Midnight. But I'm going tonight to blow up the explosives and kill the little rat…So, as I was saying. I'm rather busy."

Ramonne turned to walk away.

"Stop!"

It was not Martin's voice.

"Halt. Halt or we shoot."

Ramonne froze. But it wasn't Colonel Samarat's threat that stopped him in his tracks.

"Good. Now put your hands in the air and slowly turn around."

Ramonne made no move. His gaze was fixed straight ahead…

Where two dark-skinned youths with school backpacks were moving toward him.

23

Mestaphel walked Abdul and Omar into the *soi*. He had explained to the boys that the change in plan would work in their favor. They would go to heaven a day earlier. Their parents would be the parents of martyrs a day earlier. Allah be praised.

God is great.

Learning of the possible intrusion into his carefully laid plans had left him no choice. Again, the face of God smiled upon him in the simple act of placing a Jamah Islamiyah cell member in the driver's seat of the taxi hired by the murdering infidel.

The parking-lot attendant at the market had known the driver—in fact, he was his brother-in-law—and when the guard's body had been discovered, he had called him on his cellphone.

It wasn't long before Mestaphel was on the roof of the Pearl Hotel watching via binoculars a very interesting meeting between the Thai taxi passenger and the Frenchman he'd 'accidentally' had a drink with the night before.

He felt the tightening of a noose and he did not like it.

The Frenchman was gone before they got to the restaurant.

Disappeared. Vanished. But the Thai was at his boat. And soon he was floating in the stinking river.

Omar and Abdul were on their own when they reached Electric Blue, the neon lighting up their wide-eyed faces: "Cold Beer, Rock 'n' Roll, Showgirls." They walked on. They were instantly assaulted. First their ears. Music blared from every door. Then their eyes. Hookers beckoned from the doorways, danced on tabletops, and talked on neon cellphones.

But they were not the wanton heathens that had been described. They were pretty young girls about their own age. They smiled and flirted. Omar tripped and Abdul held his breath.

Nothing exploded, and he helped him to his feet.

They moved on down the street. They'd been prepared. They'd been trained. They were warriors. Abdul and Omar tried to remain focused. But with every step into the zone the assault accelerated.

———

Hasheem and Kahlid, however, managed to get into the target area less fazed.

Their guide escorted them into the zone from Surawong under a sign innocuously marking the area as "Pavilion Place." A KFC stood on one side, giving the area a sense of respectability, matched by its hamburger counterpart at the other end. The first fifty meters were no problem. Tailor shops. Ceramic dealers. An Internet café.

But then it got weird. They were being approached by touts with little pictures offering "massage," "young girls," "sexy lady." They shrugged them off. A little further and they met their first hooker. She was seventeen. Same as they were.

Hasheem gripped the strap of his backpack. Kahlid looked at his watch. "We have time. One beer before we go."

Hasheem had never had a beer. He thought about this and

decided he should taste the infidel's poison at least once while he was on this side. He took the pretty dyed-blonde girl's hand and sat on a barstool.

The beer was delicious. It had a musk of hops and grains, a freshness that all the tea he'd consumed in his short life had never offered. He swallowed it with gusto. He wanted more.

"Hasheem. No. We must go."

Hasheem looked at the girl. Looked at the empty glass.

"One more?" she purred.

Kahlid spit in her face.

The girl screamed and the boys hastily threw some baht on the counter and departed.

———

Ramonne moved. As he did, he heard the gun go off. The slug hit him in the shoulder. It was like a bee sting. He ignored it and lunged toward the boys. As he did, a barrage of bullets rippled through him. The force of these staggered him. He spun around.

"Martin," he hissed. "Stop them."

Martin stared. Open mouthed.

"Martin!" Ramonne commanded. "There. The boys. They are the ones."

Martin looked to where Ramonne pointed. Two terrified youths were frozen in their tracks. He looked back to Ramonne. "I-I—"

Ramonne leaped. In an instant he was gone.

"Lord Buddha," Samarat gasped.

"*Now*? Now do you believe me?" Martin asked.

Two officers held pedestrian traffic. The boys were first in line.

"Can we go?" Kahlid asked.

"Let them through," Manat instructed and reverted his gaze to the rooftops.

In the Music Café the Filipino band was kicking off their cover of Tata Young's disco hit "Sexy, Naughty, Bitchy Me." Black berets sat atop the heads of the young girls and boys who prowled the Flintstone-like faux cave interior, looking for drink orders. Omar and Abdul had given up waiting for Hasheem and Kahlid and decided to take their positions.

Mestaphel walked briskly past the countless *tuk-tuk* and taxi drivers. He shrugged off wave after wave of massage-parlor touts.

He looked at his watch. Five minutes. *Five minutes to glory.* He was almost at the van.

A hand spun him around.

"*Bonjour.*" Ramonne grinned.

"You."

"Why is everyone so surprised? Yes. Of course it's me…Time to die."

Ramonne reached for the terrorist's throat when—

A burst from a fully automatic rifle ripped through him.

"Not again."

His body was ratcheted by the gunfire, and the startled Mestaphel slipped from his grasp.

Ramonne spun around to face his attackers. The splinter core of cops numbered just three. But they were well armed. People were diving for cover as Ramonne walked back to confront them. They opened fire, but Ramonne proceeded undaunted through the hail of gunfire. He reached the first man and ripped the smoking weapon from his grasp. He used it as a club to bludgeon first one and then the rest.

Suddenly all was quiet—relatively—again.

Mestaphel was running down Silom Road. Ramonne leaped and was upon him.

"Stop."

How many times am I going to hear that tonight?

Mestaphel had a cellphone in his grasp.

Ramonne stopped.

"You know what this is for, don't you?"

Ramonne did. Punching one number would set off the bombs.

"Stop!"

It was Martin again. But this time it was directed at Manat. The two boys had just started to walk past him.

"Stop those boys."

Samarat was puzzled. "What? What are you talking about?"

Hasheem and Kahlid's eyes grew wide with fear.

"Please, sir. We've done nothing. Just let us pass."

"Check their backpacks."

"This is nonsense. We have a serious threat on our hands. We don't have time for this."

Frustrated, Martin made a move toward Hasheem. The boy panicked and undid the strap to his pack, letting it fall to the ground. Instinctively Kahlid covered his face.

Nothing happened.

Hasheem tried to run but Martin grabbed him.

Manat turned his gun on Kahlid.

"You. Take off your pack."

Shaking, the boy undid the strap. Gingerly he handed it to the officer next to him.

"Open it. Carefully," Samarat commanded.

The officer put the pack gently on the ground. He took out his knife and cut through the two straps on the top. With the flat of the blade he carefully raised the flap.

The explosive mechanism was exposed.

"It's a bomb."

"Get it out of here," Samarat ordered.

"Where shall we take it?"

Samarat thought for a moment—and then he looked up. "There. Take it to the apartment…And call the bomb squad."

———

Dozens of vendors, cabbies, and *tuk-tuk* drivers scrambled to give Ramonne and Mestaphel room as they faced off in the middle of Silom Road, right in front of the main entrance to Patpong.

There were cries of "police" from the crowd that had started to gather.

Ramonne stared at Mestaphel's hand. He calculated the possibility of lunging at the man. It was too dangerous. His finger was poised to set off the charges.

Ramonne stalled. "Why do you wish to die?"

"I…? I will not die. The infidels in their dens of sin. They will die."

"You're wrong. You *will* die. I will kill you."

Mestaphel drew a pistol.

"I don't think so."

He fired point-blank at Ramonne.

Once. Twice. Three times.

Ramonne was buffeted by the slugs, but he remained standing.

"Who *are* you?"

Ramonne smiled.

"Your executioner."

He started forward.

Mestaphel waved the phone. "Stay back, devil. I warn you."

Ramonne stopped. He was getting very annoyed with this man. And his body was smarting from the barrage of gunfire he'd recently received. "We both know you *will* set off those bombs. That is no longer a threat. You also now know that I *will* kill you. So let's make a deal."

"A deal?"

"A deal. Put down the phone, and I won't kill you."

Mestaphel scoffed. "You think I care about my life?"

"I *know* you do. I read your mind. That's why you send innocent boys to do your dirty work."

"Are these yours?" A voice came from behind Ramonne.

Mestaphel's eyes grew wide.

Ramonne turned around. Martin was walking toward them, followed by Areeya and a phalanx of police. Hasheem and Kahlid walked in front of the cops, their hands cuffed behind their backs.

"Hasheem, Kahlid! What have you done?"

"They knew about us. They took our packs."

A huge crowd was now gathered and the police had to spread out in order to keep them back. The bars and tourist stalls were emptying out as necks strained to see what was happening.

"Put down your weapon."

There were a half-dozen rifles aimed at Mestaphel.

Ramonne looked to Martin and Samarat. "That phone will detonate the bombs. There are two more boys. Two more bombs."

"Find them," Samarat barked at Manat.

Mestaphel grinned. "It is time."

As he spoke, Martin scanned the crowd. He spotted two dark-skinned young men. Omar and Abdul.

"There!"

Ramonne followed his gaze.

The boys were thirty feet away. Omar grabbed Abdul's hand.

Ramonne looked to Mestaphel, who saw the boys. He smiled.

Ramonne looked to Martin…and then to Yaya.

The two boys panicked and ran into the middle of the street.

Ramonne made a decision. He turned back to the boys and leaped.

Mestaphel also made a decision. His finger pressed the button. The cellphone lit up.

Ramonne flew through the air.

Manat fired. The bullet hit Mestaphel right between the eyes.

Ramonne landed on top of the two startled boys and crushed them to the pavement.

Two simultaneous explosions went off.

———

One blast tore off the top floor of the apartment building in Patpong 2. Windows were shattered for three blocks, and a thirty-foot fireball rained flaming debris, setting off a half-dozen other fires.

The other explosion obliterated Ramonne and the two boys, knocking over taxicabs, sending *tuk-tuks* flying through the air, and even causing a passing skytrain to jump off track and come to a screeching halt. Bloody debris was scattered for fifty yards.

Martin and Areeya were knocked to the tarmac along with everyone else. Smoke and ash filled the air, and all was eerily silent for a very long minute. And then the sounds came. The cries, the sobs…the screams.

Martin was on top of Areeya. When he finally moved, he was covered in debris and his shirt was on fire. He beat out the flames and then turned to her.

"Are you okay?"

"Yes. I think so."

Martin looked around him. Slowly, people were getting to their feet. He helped Areeya to get up. The police were checking each other before seeking to help the injured.

Sirens began to get closer as fire trucks and ambulance pick-up trucks fought to get to the scene.

Samarat walked by Martin and went to the spot where Ramonne had tackled the two boys. A six-foot circle of fire was all that was left. It was unrecognizable as the remains of three people.

Behind them, a thick cloud of black smoke rose into the night air from the burning apartment building. Sirens could be heard in the distance.

Samarat looked around. There were a lot of injuries, but he could discern no immediate fatalities. He shook his head and wiped something from his eyes.

Holding Areeya's hand, Martin slowly approached Samarat, who was staring at the ring of fire.

"Your *friend* saved a lot of people tonight," the colonel said.

Friend. Martin thought about the word. He'd used it himself once, long ago, to describe the vampire. And now, as then, it seemed appropriate.

Samarat wiped the ash on his face. "I guess we'll never know *what* he was."

Martin smiled.

He *knew.* He was his friend.

EPILOGUE

Fireworks lit up the sky above the Grand Palace. On the stage built on the riverside, a beautiful girl in full Khmer wardrobe, including a golden headdress, kissed the handsome bare-chested warrior and the curtain came down.

The pageantry of the Festival of Kings was an annual event, and for the glitterati of Bangkok society, an excuse to don their finest and board luxury boats and wine and dine on the Chao Phraya River while being treated to a historic play staged with all the pomp and circumstance that royal sponsorship could provide. The king's own barges—each with its slender profile and gilded countenance—were used as props to add authenticity to the performance, and the Grand Palace's golden spires were lit as a backdrop.

On a night such as this, Bangkok truly lived up to its *nom de plume* 'Venice of the East,' as beautiful teak yachts and specially fitted barges anchored for the performance. When it was finished, the river was an aquatic version of Rodeo Drive in Beverly Hills, with sleek and expensive boats making their departures.

Martin and Areeya were in a Chris-Craft. Its polished mahogany deck reflected the multitude of torches that lined the dock adjacent to the riverside arena. He, at her insistence, wore a tuxedo, and she had on a strapless evening gown. He had yet to give his captain the signal to cast off. They stayed in the stern, wrapped in each other, while around them the departing crafts caused the boat to ride the swell of their wakes.

"Hmmm. This is lovely."

"It is, isn't it?" Martin's face was red in the glare of the final grand burst of fireworks.

He looked at Areeya. Her rich, black hair was piled and clipped back in a fashionable bob. He leaned down and kissed her neck. She sighed and pulled him to her lips. They sank back into the satin cushions.

After a while they emerged.

"This is decadent."

"Yes, it is," Martin agreed.

"I could get used to it."

"I've been used to it. Believe me, it gets old."

"Indulge me, Martin. Spoil me. Just a little. Okay?"

He kissed her again. "Just a little. Tonight."

"And tomorrow?"

"And tomorrow we fly to Siem Reap and set up a Cambodian orphanage in his name."

She looked up at him.

"That is so cool. In a way that's as decadent as anything I could dream up."

Martin smiled, curious. "How so?"

"An orphanage. Endowed by a vampire."

"I beg your pardon. A vampire's *benefactor*. It *is* my money."

"Sorry. Correction. A vampire's benefactor. That is so cool. Come here."

They settled back into the cushions.

The captain decided to take his own lead and motioned to the deck hand to cast off. The boy unfurled the guide line and the craft slowly motored up the river. It joined a long line of similar crafts. From stem to stern they were adorned with tiny white lights, reinforcing once more the old adage that it was always Christmas in Thailand.

They passed under the Taksin Bridge. A lone figure watched them from a perch midway to the top of a far piling. The breeze blew through his dark mane, revealing a single silver stripe. As the boat moved down the river, he threw his head back and emitted a low, softly serene sound. Not a cry. Not a wail.

But a call of hope.

ABOUT THE AUTHOR

Jim Newport is a writer and Emmy-nominated production designer of both film and television. His film credits include *Bangkok Dangerous*, *Brokedown Palace*, *The Stepfather* and *Heart Like A Wheel*. In television he has set the "look" for many series by designing the pilot episodes of *The Lyon's Den*, *The Shield*, *The Education Of Max Bickford* and *China Beach*. His work on *The Piano Lesson* for the Hallmark Hall Of Fame was nominated for an Emmy in art direction. He was the production designer of season four of the worldwide hit TV series *Lost*. When not writing books or designing films, Newport performs as his alter-ego Jimmy Fame—a blues shouter, known to haunt the saloons and annual Blues Festival of his adopted home, Phuket, Thailand.

Please visit the author's website: www.vampireofsiam.com.

THE VAMPIRE OF SIAM SERIES

"These books are rich in cinematic imagery… and fascinating details of Thai history."

— THAILAND TATLER

The Vampire of Siam series is an epic tale that spans half the globe and a course of 150 years.

In *The Vampire of Siam* (Book 1) a nineteenth-century explorer, Ramonne Delacroix, encounters an ancient Chinese demon in the temples of Angkor Wat. His subsequent nocturnal transformation leads him to the capital of Siam, where he witnesses the coronation of kings and the city's metamorphosis into the modern day sin-city of Bangkok.

Living the life of the lone hunter for the first 145 years of his incarnation as a night stalker, the vampire is reborn in *Ramonne* (Book 2) and eventually seeks to know the true extent of his powers. As he learns, he evolves. By the second book's end, the vampire's strength is enormous and he has control of the true magic he has been vested with.

In *The Reckoning* (Book 3) Ramonne, armed with newfound knowledge, seeks the source of his powers. He journeys back to Cambodia and the ancient temples to a fateful encounter with Zhoupeng—the mighty devil who "turned him" so many years before. Ramonne vows to put an end to Zhoupeng's reign of evil over the poor land.

Throughout the three books, Ramonne's fate is inextricably entwined with that of Martin Larue—wealthy American expat. Drawn to each other by mutual admiration and fascination, they eventually end up relying on each other to sort out the twisted path they find themselves thrust upon.

Together they face vampire-hunters, corrupt cops, opium dens, bordellos, blind fortune-tellers, jealous lovers, terrorists, suicide-bombers, smugglers, warlords and soul-sucking demons.

The Siamese Connection (Book 4) begins in 1948 Bangkok, shortly after the end of WWII and the Japanese occupation of Siam. The vampire, Ramonne Delacroix becomes involved in a quest for a mysterious artifact—The Oracle—hidden during the war by the Japanese. He joins forces with the famous American Expat Jim Thompson, (before he was the Silk King he was an OSS agent) and together they do battle with the nefarious Japanese Black Dragons.

The tale continues in the present day picking up where *The Reckoning* left off. Martin Larue and his pregnant wife Areeya cross paths again with the vampire and soon they too are involved in a deadly game of cat and mouse with the descendants of the Black Dragons, who are still in search of the mysterious Oracle.

A fast-paced blend of fact and fiction, *The Siamese Connection* finally solves the mysterious disappearance of Jim Thompson.

"Newport artfully shapes the vampire legend into a Mekong cocktail of surprises." Christopher G. Moore.

CHASING JIMI

Chasing Jimi is a rock 'n' roll period piece. It spans one year - the summer of 1966 to the summer of 1967. From New York's Greenwich Village to swinging London to the stage of the Monterey Pop Festival. It follows the ascension of one Jimmy James, a struggling back-up guitar player, to the exalted throne of rock-god superstardom.

On the road through merry-old England with the re-named Jimi Hendrix we meet the madcap royalty of the British pop scene. Jimi forms an endearing friendship with Rolling Stones founding member Brian Jones, whose battles with numerous personal demons and plunge from the top mirror Jimi's rise and fascination with the drug culture.

As the Jimi Hendrix Experience gains recognition, Jimi's past associations throw their own stumbling blocks in his path. Contracts signed by him as a hungry studio session musician surface. Jimi's management team are able to put out most of these fires, but one particularly sleazy New York record producer refuses to be bought out, and even goes so far as to send a couple of Brooklyn wiseguys to London to bring back his artist.

Chasing Jimi is "The Sopranos" meets The Beatles. The author's intense admiration for Jimi Hendrix, his own magical experiences as a hippy in the great Summer of Love and a stint as a touring rock 'n' roll photographer in the 70s served as inspiration for Chasing Jimi.

Knowing the scrutiny he would be under for daring to write a fictional piece about Jimi, the author strived to be as accurate as possible in the timeframe of events. Liberties were taken, but they were taken in order to craft what hopefully is an amusing and entertaining tale that transports the reader back to a better time.

"Did you miss the 1960s? This funny, yet loving and respectful adventure mystery about the decade's electric sugar stud will take you back."

— JERRY HOPKINS, AUTHOR OF *THE DOORS: NO ONE HERE GETS OUT ALIVE.*

TINSEL TOWN: ANOTHER ROTTEN
DAY IN PARADISE

"Tinsel Town is the best introduction-to-Hollywood novel I've ever read."

— DAVID GILER, PRODUCER/WRITER *ALIEN*,
UNDISPUTED, MYRA BRECKINRIDGE AND
MANY MORE.

A Hollywood novel by an author who has been there - done that. Jim Newport is an Emmy-nominated production designer of both film and television. His experiences in the early years of his career served as the inspiration for Tinsel Town.

Memoirs from those in the film trade are nothing new. The bookshelves are crowded with star biographies—directors, writers and producers offering to show how difficult and arduous it is to either direct, write or produce a movie. But Tinsel Town is no simple straightforward autobiography. Like Chasing Jimi, it is a work of 'faction' - combining fact and fiction. Tinsel Town doesn't gloss over the cracks in the scenery —the grit, the stench, the plain old-fashioned blood and sweat that making movies was really about in the wild and woolly Easy Rider days of independent filmmaking. A non-stop party.

Art student Joey Morton arrives in Hollywood in 1968 and stumbles onto a sound stage. It was everything a young New Yorker could possibly hope to find—sex, drugs, gorgeous women, backstage passes, access to movie stars, rock 'n' roll... and more sex and drugs.

The author not only gives the reader a glimpse into what it

was like to enter this privileged profession in arguably its most exciting time (when movies played out in front of your own star-struck eyes, rather than against a green screen to be digitally composited later), but he also spins a tale, unravels a mystery, and takes the reader on an adventure.

"Newport's novels succeed in their purpose … they entertain."

— THE NATION.

"It moves like a runaway asteroid." Tim Hallinan, bestselling author of the Poke Rafferty series (set in Bangkok).

— TIM HALLINAN, BESTSELLING AUTHOR OF
THE POKE RAFFERTY SERIES (SET IN
BANGKOK).